MW01193327

Sins of My Youth

A Charlie McClung Mystery

By Mary Anne Edwards

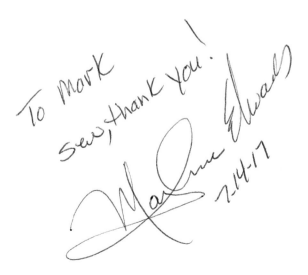

To mark
Sew, thank you!
Mary Anne Edwards
7-14-17

Publisher: CreateSpace Independent Publishing Platform

ISBN-13 978-1530085385

ISBN-10 1530085381

Cover Design by Theo Wasserberg

www.MaryAnneEdwards.com

To my husband, Jeff, for making my world complete.

I want to give a special thank you to Gina, my forever best friend, for her unending friendship and superb medical knowledge. Also, thank you to Melissa for her pathology and forensic wisdom, to my father-in-law, retired Chief Mike Edwards, and to my parents, Mingo & Peggy Gonzales for their prayers. A very special thank you to my beta readers, Judy Mackintosh and Shelby Culbertson. THANK YOU!

Also by Mary Anne Edwards

Brilliant Disguise

A Good Girl

Criminal Kind

Lyman County Georgia

Saturday, October 16, 1982

Chapter 1

"You stupid heifer! Do you honestly think I'm afraid of you?" The tall, aging David Cassidy wannabe with a stupid grin on his face, swaggered toward Joan Delaney, as her hand rested on a slightly curved filet knife.

The petite blonde laughed. "I'm not scared of you. You're not dealing with the spineless infatuated girl that you used to know." Joan wondered how she had ever found Mitch Quinn handsome and irresistible as she looked up at him; his six-foot frame towering over her barely five-foot frame. He was still in good shape but the many years of alcohol and cigarette abuse had ravaged his skin, making him look as if he were ready to retire instead of his true age of forty-six.

He stood over her, leaned down and smelled her hair. "Still miss your sweet kisses, baby."

Joan clinched the knife lying on the preparation table behind her, wanting to carve out his rotten heart and serve it to him with a sprig of parsley. Instead, she smiled. "Well, you'll never know how much sweeter they are now."

She heard the kitchen's double doors squeak. "Andrew, I ordered everyone to stay out until … this person left," Joan's head jerked toward Mitch.

Andrew stood his ground. Even though he'd only worked three months for Joan, he was fiercely loyal to her. She treated him with respect and kindness when most people could not see beyond his past.

Mitch studied Andrew, scowled at him, and then chuckled at the man fifteen years his junior. "Boy, you need to stop sniffing around her. She's way out of your league, son."

Andrew took a step forward.

Joan glared at the waiter.

He froze. His hands clenched into tight fists. "Sorry, Miss Delaney, I wanted to know if you needed any help."

Joan smiled at the stocky man with the rough exterior and kind eyes.

Andrew relaxed.

"Pfft! Miss Delaney?" Mitch looked at Joan and chuckled, "Barbie, how many times have you been married?"

Her smile froze, anger pulled at her eyes as she gripped the knife tighter. "Andrew, thank you, but I can handle this. Go see if Marian and McClung need anything."

"Yes, ma'am." The waiter frowned at Mitch then pushed through the double doors, returning to the dining room of The Primrose Cottage.

As soon as Andrew cleared the doors, Joan released the knife and pushed Mitch away. "My name is not Barbie and you know it!"

The older man rubbed his chest and laughed. "Still a little spitfire." He walked around the industrial kitchen, looking but not touching anything. "Yeah, Joan, but everyone loved Barbie, even that little boy waiter gotta crush on you. Yeah, everybody still loves Barbie." Mitch looked over his shoulder for his ex-wife's reaction.

She picked up the knife.

He turned around and threw up his hands, yellow teeth exposed as he faked a grimace of terror. "Hey now, no need for violence."

"What do you want and don't tell me after all these years it's just a 'hey, how are you' visit?" She carefully placed the knife back on the cutting board with a thick filet mignon that needed to be butterflied for one of the guests who wanted it cooked well done.

Mitch scratched the stubble on his cheek. "Well, yeah, you're right." He moved in closer to Joan, stopping just outside of striking distance. "I'm in need of some help, not much, but I figured now that you're the owner of this mighty fine establishment," Mitch waved his hand around the large brightly lit kitchen, "and I hear tell your last husband … what number was he? Three?" He shrugged. "Anyway, I understand the old geezer was a bit of a cash-cow, left you sittin' pretty high in the tax bracket, if ya know what I mean."

"And exactly why do you think that out of all the people on God's green Earth, I, the stupid heifer, would help you out?"

He studied a short stainless steel canister filled with frilly toothpicks, selected a blue one, and then held it up. "Do you mind? I must compliment your talents as a chef. Don't want to waste one tiny morsel." Mitch picked and sucked on his teeth, never taking his eyes away from Joan. "Like I was saying, I'm in a jam and I thought since we were once, you know, in love, that possibly you could remember the good times we had and help me out in this time of need."

Joan rolled her eyes. "Is that what you call it, love? Really?" She shook her head. "What's the matter? In too deep with your bookie?"

Mitch hunched up his shoulders, the stupid grin still on his leathery face.

"No," she answered calmly. "Now will you please leave? I have a hundred guests out there celebrating the marriage of my dearest friends and I don't recall you being on the guest list. Weasel your way out of my restaurant the same way you got in."

"Yeah, I know who this party is for, acting chief of police and his mighty fine, upstanding philanthropist wife: Charlie and Marian McClung." Mitch tapped his graying temple. "I still have connections. And I don't think you would want your highfalutin pals knowing about your life as Barbie, now would you?"

Joan narrowed her eyes wishing her looks could kill. "How much?"

Mitch's grin widened. "Mhm, I thought that might get that lovin' feelin' back. Fifty-thousand."

A small squeak of a laugh escaped from Joan. "You must be kidding me."

"Nope."

"You're serious?"

"Yep."

"You honestly think I'm going to give you fifty-thousand dollars, just like that?" She snapped her fingers.

Mitch shrugged, "Well, I didn't think you'd hand it to me tonight, but if you could that would be just dandy. I'm a patient and logical man. I can wait until tomorrow."

"Boy, you're more stupid than you look. I don't have that kind of money lying around," Joan chuckled. "Tomorrow is Sunday. If, and I stress if, I decide to loan you the money, I'd need to go to the bank."

Mitch tossed the used toothpick on the floor, pulled out another blue one from the canister, then pointed it at her. "Nope. There's no thinking about it. It's either yes or no but I'm a fair man. I'll give you—," He looked at his knock-off Rolex watch. "It's about ten-thirty now. You have until midnight to make up your mind and then it's, hello, Mister and Missus Charlie McClung, let me tell you a story about a girl named Barbie who you know as Joan Delaney."

"Fine! I'll meet you outside. Go out the front entrance, turn right, and then follow the path to the third bench. I'll meet you there at midnight with my decision."

"I know you'll make the right one." Mitch walked over to another preparation station. "Hmm, I like red bell peppers." He picked up a thin strip, winked at her, and then slid it into his mouth.

As her hand rested on the razor sharp knife, Joan watched him inspect each station on his way toward the walk-in freezer.

Mitch pulled on the heavy stainless door, a burst of frigid air smacked his face. "Ooo, nicely stocked and big enough to hold a side of beef I see." He smirked as he nodded. "Impressive. Very impressive, Bar—, I mean Miss Delaney."

She wanted to shove him into the freezer and lock the door behind him, leaving him in there for eternity. She knew he would never leave her alone. Mitch would bleed her dry if she gave him the money, but she didn't want anyone to know about her life as Barbie the stripper and everything else that went on during that nightmare. There had to be a way to get rid of him permanently.

A noise from the back of the kitchen caught her attention. It came from the walk-in pantry.

Joan looked at Mitch. "You wait right there." She jogged to the small storage room; the door was ajar. Flinging it open, there stood her newest waitress, Heather Neeley, hired two weeks ago. The young woman normally wore a constant smile as if she knew a coveted secret. Joan had wondered if Heather's dull brown hair was pulled back too tight in the ponytail she sported. Now a look of sheer terror replaced her ever-present smile. "What are you doing here? I told everyone to leave the kitchen."

"I was in here. The door was shut. I didn't hear you tell everyone to leave and when I opened the door, I heard you tell Andrew to get out, I froze." Heather shook, on the verge of tears.

"What did you hear? Anything?"

"No, ma'am. Nothing, I swear." Heather clasped her hands in prayer against her chest. "Please don't fire me. I need this job. My boyfriend walked out on me and my baby." Now the girl cried. "Please, I beg you. I didn't hear nothing." Heather covered her face with her hands and sobbed. "Please don't fire me. I need this job. I need it."

Joan pulled a linen napkin from one of the shelves. "Here, dry your eyes. I'm not going to fire you."

Heather grabbed Joan's hands and kissed them. "Thank you, Miss Delaney. Thank you. I'll work extra hard. You won't regret it."

6

"I know you're a good girl. Now go straighten yourself up; guests out there need your attention. Go on."

Heather squeezed Joan's hands before releasing them. "Thank you." The young girl, barely out of high school, rushed out of the kitchen, avoiding eye contact with Joan's ex-husband.

Joan followed her out of the pantry and watched her leave the kitchen. Mitch strolled around like a health inspector. "Will you please leave my kitchen? I need to get back to my job."

He stood in front of her. With his index finger, he tilted up her chin, his lips almost touching her. "Just one for old-times' sake?"

Joan smelled his alcohol, cigarette-laced breath as it washed over her face. This time she grabbed the knife and held the point to his neck. A pinprick of blood bloomed from his Adam's apple. "Get out!"

Mitch calmly backed away as he touched his neck, and then looked at the bright red stain on his fingertips. "Now there was no need for this. What would your buddies, the McClungs, think about this?" He held up his bloody fingers. "Tsk-tsk. You're still a bad girl but not the kind of bad girl you used to be."

"I said, get out! Now!"

Laughing, he strolled toward the set of double doors. Mitch put his hand on one of them, turned to face Joan, and with the other hand, the one with the bloody fingers, saluted her as he clicked his tongue. "I'm looking forward to our midnight rendezvous … Barbie."

With the knife in her hand, Joan took a few quick steps toward her first ex-husband. "My name is Joan. Do you understand? It's always been Joan!"

7

Mitch placed his clean hand over his heart. "You'll always be my sweet baby girl, Barbie." He walked out the double doors, the stupid grin still on his face.

Chapter 2

Marian looked around the dining room of The Primrose Cottage. Her best friend in the entire world, Joan, was hosting, as she called it, a post-honeymoon bliss party. She had insisted Joan keep it small and simple. The crowd was small but the food was beyond compare, as usual. Charlie's parents, Ma and Da, were the only in-laws that had been able to make it, but she knew she'd see the whole family at Christmas.

Ma spoke to Miss Joyce, probably about recipes. Miss Joyce was the only baker who could rival Joan's skills. Her cakes and pies graced the glass display case at the entrance of The Primrose Cottage.

"Charlie, do you know that man over there?" Marian pointed discreetly toward Mitch Quinn standing at the bar of The Primrose Cottage.

Her husband of exactly one month and five days, sipped an ice-cold glass of diet Dr Pepper. Detective Charlie McClung looked at the older man. "Not really. He introduced himself to me as one of Joan's friends. Said his name is Mitch Quinn."

"Hmm, strange, he introduced himself to me too, and gave us his best wishes. He also commented on Joan's success. But I don't recall

Joan ever mentioning someone by that name." She took the slender glass from Charlie's hand, and then drank. "I wonder why she invited him. He must mean something to her."

"Hmm." Marian held the glass to her lips. "But then again, Joan considers her past too dull and boring to waste her breath on." She drained the glass. "Which is fine. I don't give a hill of beans about her past."

Charlie took the empty glass from his bride's hand. "Would you like a glass of your own?

"What?"

Charlie shook the glass. The ice cubes made a pretty tinkling sound.

Marian blushed. "Oh, sorry about that. I guess a glass of my own would be nice." She kissed his cheek. "You're the best."

Her husband grinned. "You're not so bad yourself." Charlie saw Mitch talking to his friend, Jack Jackson, the medical examiner. "I'll be back in a few."

"Hmm, I don't think so. I see that look in your eyes and I see who's standing at the bar. You're in detective mode." Marian blew him a kiss. "Go, have fun. I need to mingle anyway."

Charlie grabbed the kiss and put it in his pocket over his heart. "Saving it." He walked toward the bar.

A shapely platinum-haired woman had latched on to Mitch, giggling like Goldie Hawn at everything he said.

Charlie thought she resembled Jayne Mansfield, except with poufy long hair flowing down her back. As he approached the trio, he noticed that Jack looked a little uncomfortable.

"Hey, Jack!" Charlie clamped his hand on his friend's thin shoulder.

"McClung, have you met Mitch and his friend, Candi?"

"Yes, I've met Mitch." He could see why Jack was nervous, as Candi leaned across Mitch and extended her hand. Charlie was afraid her breasts would spill out of the low-cut shimmering white dress she wore.

"Charmed, I'm sure," Candi purred.

Charlie felt her fingers lightly tickle his palm as they shook hands. He felt violated by her leer.

Mitch rubbed her forearm. "Calm down, Candi. He's acting chief of police."

Candi's sensuous ogle instantly became a virtuous smile, as she promptly withdrew her hand.

"Candi, that's an interesting name. Are you a performer?" Charlie motioned for the bartender.

"Yeah, she's quite the performer." Mitch slapped her butt.

Candi giggled. "I'm an artistic dancer."

Charlie's left eyebrow arched at her fanciful way of saying she was a stripper.

"Another diet Dr Pepper for you sir?" The bartender reached for a glass, ready to fill it.

"No, make it a regular Dr Pepper." Charlie addressed the trio. "Anything for you? I'm buying and I have taxis waiting to drive you home."

Mitch patted Charlie's back. "Now you are definitely my kind of cop." He threw back his drink. "Another Wild Turkey."

Candi clapped her hands as she jumped up and down; her breasts tried to escape. "A strawberry wine cooler, please." She peeked around Mitch. "Thank you … what was your name?'

"McClung, you can call me McClung." Charlie averted his eyes away from the giggling woman's indecent exposure.

"Thank you, McClung. I just adore strawberry wine coolers."

Charlie turned to Jack. "Refill on your beer?"

"Nah, Joan and I are going to talk after your soiree is over. I don't want to be drunk."

Charlie nodded to the bartender. "I think that's it for the order."

"Yes, sir."

Mitch snorted. 'Be careful of that one, Jack. She's dangerous."

"What do you—?"

Charlie held up his hand. "Jack, I've got this."

"Sure."

"Mitch, exactly how do you know Joan?"

The bartender returned quickly with their drinks since they were the only ones at the bar. Most of the guests were still enjoying the elaborate buffet Joan and her staff had prepared. Desserts and coffee had been brought out an hour ago.

Mitch grinned and sipped his fresh glass of bourbon. "Well, Joan and I go back a long way. I'd say about twenty-one years." He took another sip. "Yep, she was once my wife."

Charlie smirked. "Is that right? Your wife."

Candi didn't react to Mitch's remark; she was too busy guzzling the wine cooler.

"Yeah, do you find it hard to believe she let someone like me slip through her fingers, or did you think she was pure as the driven snow?"

Charlie pointed to a piece of white tissue with a bright red center stuck to Mitch's neck. "How did you get that cut? It looks fresh."

Mitch removed the speck of paper, rolled it between his fingers, and then flicked it somewhere behind the bar. "I said she was dangerous."

"Are you saying Joan did that?"

Joan's first ex-husband smirked and tossed back his bourbon.

Marian slid up between Mitch and Charlie. "So sorry to interrupt but I want to introduce you to Rocky. He's one of the caregivers at Haven House." She looked at Mitch. "You don't mind if I steal my husband away, do you?"

"Nope, not at all." He looked at his watch. "I've gotta meet someone in a few minutes." Mitch looked at Jack. "Do you mind keeping Candi entertained until I return?"

Jack blinked a few times and swallowed.

Mitch walked over to Jack, slapping him on the back. "Ah, she won't bite unless you want her to." Mitch chuckled. "Just keep the wine coolers coming and you'll be all right."

"Thank you, Mitch." Marian looked at the drunk woman. "I don't think we've met. I'm Marian McClung."

"Charmed, I'm sure. My name's Candi, with an i," she slurred, quickly dismissing Marian. She wiggled her finger at the bartender and held up her empty bottle. "I would like another one, plea—," Candi hesitated. "Wait. Who's paying for my drinks?" She looked at Mitch.

"Baby, I've gotta meet someone at midnight, remember?"

Candi stared unblinking. "Yeah, but who's buying me drinks?"

"Jack's going to, right?"

Jack shrugged, "I guess?"

Candi grinned stupidly. "Thank you, Jacky boy."

"Well Mitch, now that's settled, Charlie and I will be leaving so you can go to your meeting." Marian whispered into Jack's ear. "We'll be back shortly to rescue you."

Mitch strolled out the entrance of The Primrose Cottage, turned right, and then followed the brightly lit curving path. The only sounds he heard were his footsteps on the flagstones and occasional crunching of the pea gravel between the stones as he made his way to the third bench as Joan had instructed. The first bench was out in the open, sitting in front of a large three-tiered water fountain surrounded by flowers. Strategically placed spotlights illuminated the area. Nothing unusual about the bench except it was U-shaped and could seat probably six adults. A concrete cat was curled up asleep underneath it.

The second bench was different from the first. It had a flat wooden seat and a tangled mess of vines for the back. This bench was a little more secluded, set back from the path in a thick clump of bright red crepe myrtles with strands of clear lights woven in the branches, a hummingbird feeder dangled from a limb. Mitch stopped. Something large fluttered around the large plate-like base of the feeder. He took a small step toward the feeder but quickly backed away.

"A bat! I hate bats," Mitch mumbled as he continued in his quest for the third bench.

Entering the forest, the lights along the pathway cast eerie shadows.

Mitch jumped when a rabbit hopped across the path. "I hate the woods, especially at night. She knows that. Stupid heifer."

"Finally! The bench." Mitch was thankful for the single gas lamp behind the third bench. He sat down on the unusual bench, the base was natural stacked stone, the seat and back were smooth concrete, painted red, and all edges were rounded.

Mitch spoke aloud to give himself courage. "I wonder when she'll get here. Joan was always late. Stupid heifer."

He leaned back and then threw his arms out, resting them on the back of the bench. "Not too bad, rather comfortable for concrete."

The sound of crickets and frogs filled the dark shadows between the oaks and pines. Soft footsteps broke the night chorus.

Mitch looked at his watch, thirteen minutes past midnight. "You're late," he shouted toward the footfalls and listened for Joan's sarcastic reply but heard nothing but the sounds of the forest.

"Hmm, my ears must be playing tricks on me." He sat in silence, listening to the sounds of the night.

Moths and other flying insects danced around the gas lamp behind the stone bench. Mitch watched their crazy shadows zigzag in front of him.

The small insect shadows were overtaken by a much larger one, that of a human.

"Well, it's about time. I was about to go find your friends and entertain them with tales of our glorious past."

He felt fingers run through his thick hair, and then massage the top of his head.

"Oh, baby, that feels good. So the flame still burns for me."

Without warning, Mitch's head was violently yanked backward and bashed against the red concrete. He felt an intense burning pain across his throat that instantly replaced the throb in his cracked skull. He tried to speak but no words came out, only a gurgle. The rhythm of his heart slowed down, making him feel tired, oh so tired. The cold concrete bench only intensified the frigidity that now engulfed his body and he wished Joan would wrap her arms around him to keep him warm. Thoughts of happier days with Joan flitted around his brain.

Mitch always knew he wouldn't live to a ripe old age, probably die from cancer due to his non-stop smoking. He thought maybe Joan had saved him from a lingering, horrible death. *But why did she send me here to die? Joan knows I hate being in the woods at night.*

Mitch closed his eyes and died.

Chapter 3

"You're alone? What happened to Candi?" Charlie thought for certain that Jack would have to be rescued from the wine cooler girl.

"Did Mitch come back for her?" Marian was relieved the two were gone. They gave her the creeps.

Jack shook his head. "Nope, as soon as Mitch went through the front door, she took off her shoes and followed him. She didn't even say thank you for the drinks or say goodbye."

"Took off her shoes, huh? I guess she didn't want Mitch to know she was following him." Charlie's curiosity was overwhelming. "Say, why don't we take a moonlight stroll?"

"You read my mind." Marian grinned as Charlie slid his arm around her waist.

Charlie looked at Jack sitting all alone. He knew Marian wanted Jack and Joan to be a couple. Their two best buds, she couldn't resist playing matchmaker. "Go find Joan. Let's all go for a stroll."

"Too late; she left after Candi went tip-toeing through the tulips."

Charlie glanced at Marian who stared up at him. He had told his wife about Mitch's revelation concerning her best friend. "Are you thinking what I'm thinking?"

"Probably, but I find it hard to believe. First, that Joan was ever married to a guy like him, and second, that she would meet him for a midnight rendezvous."

"Let's go then." Charlie looked at Jack. "Are you coming with us?"

"I don't want to be the third wheel and I certainly don't want to see Mitch and Joan together." Jack waved at the bartender and held up his empty beer mug. "I'll just numb my emotions and then take a cab home."

Marian moved over to Jack. "Don't let your imagination get the best of you. We don't know for certain Mitch and Joan are hooking up." She rubbed his narrow back. "Joan may have stepped outside to decompress. This party took a lot of planning and work on her part. She refused to let me help."

"I know you're probably right but if it's all the same, I'll sit here and think." Jack drank from the frosty mug the bartender had just put before him.

Charlie wanted Jack to be happy but he knew there was nothing he could do about it right now. He tugged on Marian's hand. "Come on. Let's go for that stroll."

Marian let Charlie lead her out the front door, and then Marian took the lead.

"When Joan and I take a walk together, we always turn right."

They had just reached the first bench when they heard a scream coming from the woods.

"That's Joan!" Marian ran toward her best friend's cry for help.

"Wait!" Charlie took after his wife. She was fast but he was faster, and his legs were longer. As he ran past Marian, he yelled at her to stay behind him.

He flew by the second bench. The screaming grew louder. At the third bench, Charlie saw Joan. She held a knife in her right hand and stared at Mitch sitting on the bench. At first glance, he appeared to be asleep. Charlie knew nothing could be done for Mitch. Joan was his biggest concern for now.

"Oh, no, Joan, are you okay?" Marian had her arm around her friend's waist. "Joan, honey, give the knife to Charlie. Okay?"

"Everything is all right, sweetie. Everything is all right." Charlie crooned as he reached out his hand, holding a tissue.

Joan's mouth was wide open as she struggled to breathe, her eyes bulging as tears streamed down her face. She heard Charlie's voice but couldn't comprehend what he wanted her to do.

Charlie gently removed the knife from Joan's tight grip, and then wrapped it carefully in tissues. He laid the bundle on the ground. "Joan, are you hurt?"

Joan stared at the white wad of tissues lying on the ground as Charlie and Marian examined her for cuts or scratches but all they found was blood. And it wasn't hers.

Charlie held Joan's forearms, trying to get her to look into his eyes, but she kept her focus on the bloody tissues. "Joan, look at me, not the ground. Do you understand? Joan!" He shook her arms.

Joan looked up at Charlie and whispered, "That's my knife." Her body shook. "That's my knife, Charlie! My knife!"

Charlie heard a twig snap. The sound came from the woods, opposite the bench.

"Marian, stay here with Joan and try to calm her down." Charlie knelt down, removed his ankle weapon, a Smith and Wesson Model 36, and then slid the small two-inch barreled gun into her right hand. "Just in case," he whispered into her ear.

She nodded, not afraid to use it if she needed to defend herself and Joan. Marian put her left arm around Joan's shoulders, turning her away from Mitch's body.

Joan cried, covering her face with her bloody hands as Marian reassured her everything would be okay.

Charlie hated to leave them alone, but someone was out there, watching. Retrieving his service revolver from his shoulder holster and a penlight from his pants pocket, he cautiously moved toward the area where the sound had come from. The light from the gas lamp barely penetrated the darkness in the trees. The penlight was a pinprick of light, useless.

He decided to turn back and have the area searched thoroughly at daybreak. A noise behind him made him turn and he strained to see through the veil of darkness. Someone was out there in the woods. Charlie wanted to go after them but knew it would be a waste of time and could even destroy evidence by stumbling around in the woods. He fought the urge to chase whoever it was and decided to return to Marian and Joan.

Exiting the trees, Charlie saw Marian talking to one of the waiters, and wondered why he was out here when he should have been at The Primrose doing his job.

"Andrew, what are you doing out here?" Charlie reached down for the knife, keeping his stare on the waiter's face.

The young man swallowed a few times before his voice came to him. His eyes darted toward Mitch's lifeless body, then back at Charlie. "Uh, I needed to ask Miss Delaney a question."

"But how did you know to look for her here?"

"Heather told me Miss Delaney was meeting that man," Andrew jerked his thumb over his shoulder toward Mitch, "out in the woods just after midnight."

Charlie believed he was concerned about Joan but knew he didn't come all the way out here just to ask her a question. Earlier in the evening, he had seen Mitch go into the kitchen, saw Andrew leave, only to return in a few minutes, and then exit again quickly. A few minutes later, Heather flew out of the kitchen. Now was not the time for an interview. He needed to preserve the crime scene and collect evidence.

"Andrew, I'm trusting you with my wife and Miss Delaney. Retrace your steps back to The Primrose but don't go through the front entrance. Go through the back kitchen entrance."

The waiter glanced at the small pistol in Marian's hand. "Yes, sir. Then what?"

Charlie looked at his watch and pressed a button to illuminate its face, almost one o'clock in the morning. The whole town should be asleep by now. "Call 9-1-1. Tell them Chief McClung said there's been a homicide at The Primrose Cottage. No sirens or flashing lights unless absolutely necessary. Can you do that? "

"Yes, sir." Andrew nodded and touched Joan's elbow. "Come with me, Miss Delaney."

She looked questioningly first at Andrew then at Marian.

"It's okay. I'm coming with you." Marian squeezed her best friend's shoulder.

Joan whispered, "Okay but …" She trembled as she glanced over her shoulder at her dead ex-husband and began to sob.

Charlie pressed a tissue into Marian's hand. She removed her arm draped around Joan's shoulders.

As Marian blotted the tears streaming down her friend's cheeks, Charlie whispered into her ear. "Once you're inside the restaurant, get Ma to stay with Joan. Ask Da and Rocky to keep everyone inside. Make sure Heather is there. I have a few questions for her. Then I want you to bring Jack here." He kissed her temple. "Get going and hurry back."

Marian nodded. "Joan, let's go get you something strong to drink."

Andrew gently gripped his boss's elbow. "Miss Delaney, let's get you back to The Primrose. You're shivering." Hesitantly, he rubbed the chill bumps on Joan's thin forearm. He glanced at Marian. "We'll get you warmed up."

Joan's stunned gaze darted from Andrew's hand on her arm to Marian's face. Her head jerked slightly, acknowledging she understood.

Charlie watched the trio trudge down the pathway. He thought Joan seemed to have shrunk, so tiny, child-like, in between Andrew, five-foot-six, and Marian, who was only five-foot-three. Tearing his attention away from his wife, he looked at Mitch's body and the immediate surrounding area, careful not to disturb anything, even footprints.

The night sounds returned, eerily filling the silence. Charlie used his pen light to augment the wavering light from the gaslight lamp behind the concrete bench. Mitch's chin rested on his chest, his hands lay on either side of his narrow thighs, knees splayed open. If it weren't for the blood-soaked shirt, you'd think Mitch was in a deep sleep.

Charlie focused the beam on Mitch's neck. He could see deep cuts on either side and was certain once the body was moved, he would discover that the incision ran from ear to ear. The wound appeared clean, deep, and professional. He looked at his hands. The nails were clean. "Hmm, no struggle," Charlie mumbled softly. Next, he gingerly stepped to the back of the bench. The ground was covered in pea gravel and large pieces of stepping stones, no visible footprints.

Blood and a few strands of hair were on the back of the bench. The penlight revealed a patch of blood-matted hair on the crown of Mitch's head. A thick tuft of gelled hair stood up in front of the wound. Charlie carefully retraced his way back to the main path. Standing guard over the grisly scene, he waited for his team and Jack to arrive.

Looking around the dark dense forest, Charlie fixed his gaze on Mitch. He listened to the sounds, sounds Mitch probably heard.

Charlie crossed his arms, and then rubbed his earlobe as he spoke softly to himself.

"Mitch was definitely waiting for someone. Joan? Hmm, whoever it was must have approached him from behind, pulled back his head, cut his throat, and then ...?"

Inhaling deeply, Charlie rubbed his face with both hands, shook his head, and then shoved his hands into his back pockets. "For Marian's sake, please don't let it be Joan."

Marian was not enjoying this usually pleasant walk through the woods toward the gardens of The Primrose. Not only was Joan bloody and a mental wreck, but it was apparent to Marian that someone was following them. She had Charlie's gun, and was ready to use it.

Andrew babbled on with Joan about tasks that needed to be addressed at The Primrose. "Miss Delaney, do you think we should break down the buffet? It is getting late. Coffee and dessert has been served. What do you think Miss Delaney?"

They heard a snap as someone carelessly stepped on a small branch, the sound echoing behind them as they exited the forest, entering open ground. Marian froze. Andrew shifted his gaze away from Joan toward her. Marian nodded to keep walking.

Lagging two steps behind, Marian turned, wishing she had the night vision of a cat. There was nothing. She quickly caught up with Joan and Andrew. Sounds from The Primrose could now be heard. Marian sighed.

"Miss Delaney, I think we should go through the kitchen's back entrance. What do you think?" Andrew squeezed his boss's red-stained hand.

Joan nodded. "Yes, Andrew, I need to …" Her voice trailed, confused by not knowing what she needed to do.

"We're going to take care of things, Joan, don't you worry, sweetie." Marian kissed her best friend's cheek.

"Hey! Wait for me!" Candi stumbled behind them.

Joan screamed and cowered in Marian's arms.

Andrew threw himself in front of them shielding the two women from the intruder. "What the hell are you doing out here running around and screaming like a crazy person?"

"Miss Delaney, Miss Marian, it's nothing to be afraid of, no danger. Okay?" The stocky young man gently patted them on their backs.

Marian stroked Joan's silky blonde hair. "It's okay, sweetie. Just a few more steps and we'll be inside. All right?"

The trio continued toward the kitchen door.

"Hey, what about me?"

They ignored Candi's demand for attention.

She trailed behind them grumbling incoherently.

Once inside the bright warm kitchen, Andrew and Marian guided Joan to her small office beside the walk-in pantry. "Joan, stay here with Andrew, okay?"

She nodded silently, staring at her hands resting limply on the monthly desk calendar filling most of the space on the desk top. The blood on her right hand was drying to a dark brownish maroon color.

As Marian held Andrew's glance, she tilted her head down toward the desk drawer; silently slid it open, set the gun inside, and then closed it. Andrew nodded in understanding.

Candi was eating black olives from one of the stainless steel preparation stations. "Andrew, I'm going to get Ma to stay with you and Joan while I take care of her," Marian said as she stabbed her finger toward Candi. "And don't forget to make that phone call."

Marian stormed out of the office, and then stopped suddenly, looking at the stripper's dirty bare feet with a scattering of bloody scratches. "Where are your shoes?"

With a black olive poised in front of her parted full lips, Candi giggled, "I dropped them at the door." She popped the olive into her mouth, and shrugged with a pleased grin.

Marian collected the stiletto platform sandals and grumbled softly, *No wonder she took these off. How in the world do you walk in these things*? She held the deathtraps in front of Candi. "Here."

"You're such a sweetie," Candi purred with a seductive look in her eyes. "Do you reckon she can get herself cleaned up and fix me something to eat? The night air seems to make me hungry." Candi batted her eyelashes at Marian.

Bamboozled by Candi selfishness, Marian snorted and gripped the stripper's boney elbow. "Well, you won't think I'm a sweetie for long." She yanked Candi away from the olives, and then dragged her out of the kitchen.

"Hey, you can't treat me like this!"

"Don't think I'm so sweet now, do you?" Marian pushed open the door which led to the main dining room.

"What do you think you're doing bitc—?"

Marian shoved Candi over toward the wait staff's nook. "Finish your sentence, and I'll have you arrested."

"You can't do that!" The stripper looked down at Marian.

"Just try me."

Candi backed away from Marian's stern matter-of-fact tone; it frightened her, memories, painful memories, memories Candi thought had died when she ran away from her mother.

"You stay right here. Don't move from this spot. Do you understand?"

Candi nodded and whispered, "Yes, ma'am," and then pressed her back against the wall.

"All right then." Marian left Candi to search for Ma and Da among the partygoers, surprised no one had left, apparently unaware of what had happened in the woods.

She found Da chatting with Rocky. "Just who I was looking for." Marian threw her arms around Da.

"What's the matter, child? Ya, look like ya been seein' a ghost." Da searched the room for his wife. He smiled. Ma's sixth sense was bringing her over.

Marian released her grip. "Da, something terrible has happened in the woods. Charlie needs you, and you too, Rocky to guard the doors. Don't let anyone leave."

Da kissed his wife's forehead, knowing his new daughter would be in good hands, and then without any questions, he and Rocky left to take their positions.

"What's troublin' ya, love?" Ma gently cradled Marian's cheeks between her soft hands.

"Charlie is okay but something bad has happened. I need you to stay with Joan. Come with me."

Ma and Marian made their way to the kitchen, passing Candi still pressed against the wall.

They entered Joan's office.

Ma gasped upon seeing Joan's blood-smeared face and hands. "Janey Mac! Are ya hurt bad, flower?"

Joan burst into tears.

"Come, darlin.'" Ma wrapped her arms around Joan and looked at Andrew. "Son, go get us a sweet sherry."

He shot out of the office.

"Ma, will you stay with her? I've got to take Jack to Charlie."

"Most certainly. Go on now, love."

At the kitchen door, Marian met Andrew carrying two glasses and a bottle of sherry. "Did you call the police?"

"Yes, ma'am. They're on the way."

Marian nodded and went to find Jack. As she stepped through from the kitchen, she heard Jack's voice. He was speaking with Candi.

"Jack!"

He turned, "What's going on? Is what she's saying true?"

Marian looked at Candi. "What did she say?"

Candi stared at her bare feet.

"She said Joan killed Mitch."

Marian grabbed Jack's hand. "I don't believe it for one second, but that's what we're going to find out. Come on, Charlie needs you. But first, I need to get something. Wait here." She released his hand and ran into the kitchen.

Jack watched the doors swing in her wake, and then almost instantly, Marian reappeared, gun in hand.

She glared at Candi, "You, don't leave the restaurant."

The young woman protested but then decided it was in her best interest not to provoke the she-bear holding a gun, so she held her tongue.

"Good. Jack, let's go."

Chapter 4

Marian gasped. The woods were glowing. "Oh, no, the forest is on fire!"

"Calm down. Do you smell any smoke?" Jack was in a hurry to get to the crime scene. Marian told him what little she knew and he agreed Joan had to be innocent. He wanted her to be innocent.

She inhaled deeply, and then laughed nervously. Marian picked up her pace to reach Charlie. The closer they got to the spot where Mitch was killed, the brighter the lights and the louder the sounds of people talking grew louder. Charlie's voice was the most dominant.

"What's all this?" Marian rubbed the small of her husband's back.

Charlie kissed her temple. "I gotta say one good thing about Chief Perry Miller, he used some of his drug money to outfit this department with everything they could possibly need in any situation."

"Really? You can keep all this stuff?" Marian saw at least twelve shop lights connected to portable generators. Bright yellow crime scene tape was strung as far as she could see.

"Yep, the anonymous donor turned out to be Perry. The court made their decision a week ago. In layman's term, the dirty money was used for the greater good, therefore, we get to keep everything." Charlie saw one of his men about to step into the forest. "Hey, Officer Willard, don't go into the forest. We're going to wait until daylight, need all the light we can get. Don't want to miss a thing."

"Yes, sir, Chief McClung," the young recruit gave Charlie a friendly salute with a smile.

Marian grinned. "Hmm, Chief McClung. You like that don't you?"

Charlie shrugged with a lopsided smirk.

She bumped her husband's shoulder with hers. "Well, I think it fits you perfectly and it's quite apparent your men admire you."

"They may not after this investigation. It's going to be non-stop."

Charlie had a way about him that made Marian feel content, at peace, but with his last words, a dark melancholy descended upon her. Marian had only known Joan for six years, but she knew, just knew, her friend didn't kill Mitch.

"Charlie, I'm going back to The Primrose to be with Joan, besides, I'll be in the way here." Marian gave her husband a quick peck on the lips.

Charlie gave a sharp whistle. His men snapped to attention. He trusted all of his men after picking out the bad seeds. "I need a volunteer to be a bodyguard for my wife."

All of the officers stepped forward.

"Well, now, I see my lovely bride has charmed you all," Charlie chuckled. "Officer Thayer, you've known her the longest."

The baby-faced officer almost jumped for joy, containing himself before his feet left the ground. He replaced his expression of elation with a more serious one befitting his duty assignment. "Yes, sir! I will protect her with my life."

"Of course you will. If anything happens to her, it will be your life."

Officer Thayer didn't even begin to smile, knowing his chief was deadly serious. "Sir, yes sir!"

Charlie kissed the top of Marian's head. "I'll join you as soon as I get everything sorted out. All right?"

"Mmhm. Do you want this back?" Marian held out his gun, muzzle toward the ground.

"No, keep it until we go home, together, all right?"

"Okay."

Charlie gave his wife a quick squeeze. "Officer Thayer, safeguard my wife."

He watched Marian and his officer until they were out of sight, said a prayer for their protection, and then turned his attention to the crime, knowing his wife was in good hands.

"Jack, what do you think happened?" Charlie watched the medical examiner.

"Well," Jack's nose was almost touching Mitch's neck as he peered at the fresh wound, "his throat was definitely slashed, ear to ear as the old cliché goes." He stood, pointing the flashlight directly on the top of Mitch's head. "Hmm, he must have used lots of hair goo."

Charlie stood next to Jack and shined his light at the clump of hair. "Yep, looks like someone grabbed his hair."

"Is it okay for me to walk around the bench?"

Charlie trained the beam of light in front of Jack's feet even though there was a spotlight flooding the area. He didn't want a speck of evidence destroyed. "Watch your step."

The two men painstakingly made their way around the bench, each footstep making crunching sounds in the pea gravel surrounding the concrete bench.

Charlie and Jack stood behind Mitch.

"I think Mitch was surprised by whoever it was that attacked him. The position of his body is too relaxed, his clothes aren't disheveled. What do you think, Jack?"

"I think you're right, but I'll need to scrape under his fingernails for any tissue, just to be sure. It appears someone grabbed his hair and yanked his head back, and then slit his throat."

"Yeah, I can see blood here," Charlie pointed to a dark spot on the top edge of the bench, "and there's a bloody patch there." He indicated the wet spot on the back of Mitch's head.

"Hmm, you see the spray pattern of the blood?" Jack followed the apparent path of the spew with the flashlight.

"Do you think the killer would have any on them?"

Jack hunched up his shoulders. "Maybe, hard to say." He sighed heavily. "You really don't think it was Joan, do you?"

Charlie rubbed his face, feeling the roughness of stubble. "For Marian's sake, I pray not, but I've been doing this long enough to know you can never rule out anyone, no matter how saintly they appear."

The surrounding forest was dark, only the outer fringe was lighter because of the strategically placed spotlights. Charlie pressed a button on his watch, illuminating the dial.

"Man, this night is dragging, only a little after three o'clock. The sun won't be up for another four hours." Charlie looked up at the thick canopy. "There won't be much sunlight filtering through that."

Jack retraced his steps back to the main path, and then studied the blood spatter. "Has your cameraman arrived?"

Charlie was studying the ground behind the bench. The last rain was three days ago, over half an inch on Wednesday, and another quarter on Thursday. He knelt down, the forest floor was still moist. There was a pattern in the dew-covered vegetation. "Good question. I could use him right now." He dusted off his hands, and then joined Jack.

Charlie walked toward his men mingling on the path. "Hey, Sam! We need you over here."

The grey-haired man trotted over, an oversized camera bag slapping against his hip as he held a camera close to his wide chest. "What cha got?"

"Ah, the usual kind of stuff, blood spatters, victim, and a trail I think the killer used." Charlie shook hands with Sam. "Jack, this is Sam, Sam Goldstein, best cameraman around here. Not only does he take stills, he's got a Panasonic color video camera."

"I'm impressed. Pleasure to meet you." Jack liked the jolly man.

The older man shrugged, "Mm, what can I say? I like to stay up on technology." Sam looked Jack over. "Are you new in the department?"

"No, sir. I'm a medical examiner."

"Come on, Jack, don't sell yourself short." Charlie gripped Jack's thin shoulder. "Sam, this man works with the Georgia Bureau of Investigation."

"Now I'm the one who's impressed." Sam pumped Jack's hand faster.

"Let's get this show on the road. Sam, I need pictures of the victim and all the surrounding area. Even under the bench, all sides."

Jack added to Charlie's list. "I need close-ups of his hands, throat, back of his head, and feet. Plus, all blood spatters, on the ground, bench, and his clothes."

Sam set down his bag, pulled out a flash, attached it to his camera, and methodically photographed the area. "Once I finish with the stills, I'll video tape the whole scene."

"Before videotaping, I need you to get shots of the path behind the bench, and then tape that area first." Charlie pointed toward the trees.

As Sam clicked away, Charlie studied the position of Mitch's body and the expression on his face, serene as if he welcomed death. The fine Italian suit was ruined by copious amounts of blood.

"Look at this, Jack. See this?"

Both men aimed their flashlights to the left of Mitch's left thigh. A faint outline of where the killer placed the knife after they slit Mitch's throat. A spray of blood droplets with larger, more line-like blood pattern in a V-shape.

"Sam, did you get this?"

He paused, looked at the place Charlie was pointing. "Yes, chief." Sam let the camera hang from his neck. "I'm finished with this area, ready for the next." He picked up the heavy camera bag.

Jack stayed with Mitch's body, while Charlie guided Sam to the wooded path.

"You see that dark line running through the moss?"

Sam handed Charlie the bag. "Mhm." The camera flashed several times as Sam zoomed in and out at various angles. "Hold the bag while I get the video out." Sam connected various contraptions to the camera, shoulder rest, lights, and cables. Satisfied, he hefted it to his left shoulder. "Action! Camera's rolling." Slowly he panned the camera around the forest floor.

Charlie tapped Sam on the shoulder, "You think you got it all?"

"Yes, chief. It would be nice to have more natural light."

"Well, yeah, but we've got a few more hours for that. Let's film the area with the body."

Jack blew on his hands to warm them. "Hey, any chance we can move the body soon?"

"As soon as Sam's finished. Go ask one of the officers to have the medics prepare to remove the body."

By the time Jack returned, Sam was ready to video tape the removal of the body.

There were no surprises. Rigor was nonexistent due to the tremendous amount of blood loss, so the removal was easy.

"I'll follow the body and begin the autopsy."

"I'm right behind you. I need to start the interviews."

Sam grunted as the weight of the camera bag settled on his shoulder. "I'll get the film processed, and then return here around seven o'clock to photograph the area in the daylight."

"Sounds like a plan." Charlie shook Sam's hand. "Jack, call me when you're done. Call the precinct, they'll know where I am."

Jack gave Charlie a two-finger saluted, turned, and followed the medics out of the forest.

Chapter 5

Charlie gave his men instructions to secure the area and not let anyone near the crime scene unless it was a direct order from himself. He made every man check their two-way radios to ensure they were on and working.

"I'll be at The Primrose gathering statements." Charlie looked at each man. "At sun up, we'll comb this whole area for any tiny bit of evidence. This is the first time anything like this has happened in Lyman County. I know I can depend on each of you to perform your duties in a professional and meticulous manner."

"Yes, sir" the men acknowledged.

Charlie smiled, pleased with the group of good men. "If anyone approaches this area, get their name, contact info, why they are here, and then send them away." He turned to leave, but decided to address his officers, "And another thing, I'll have coffee and biscuits sent to you."

The men cheered, thanking their chief.

"Keep your eyes and your ears peeled for anyone lurking in the forest. The killer could be out there watching."

Officer Willard stepped forward. "Sir, if someone approaches and then flees when we advance toward them, should we pursue and apprehend the suspect?"

Charlie rubbed his chin. "Good question. If you know the person, don't bother, just make a note of it. We'll talk with them later. But a stranger, yes, two of you will follow the perpetrator. Don't go alone."

"Yes, sir."

"Any more questions?"

Silence.

"Good. Coffee and biscuits are on the way."

The hair on Charlie's neck stood to attention. Someone was following him, someone in the forest, and from the sound of their footfalls snapping twigs and booting stones, someone big and clumsy. His hand was poised over his revolver. Whoever it was, was not trying to hide the fact they were following him. Which meant they intended no harm or were not afraid of being caught. But why were they trailing him?

Once out of the trees and into the open garden, Charlie could no longer hear his stalker. He knelt down, pretended to check his shoe lace, glanced under his armpit, and then as he stood, stretched and turned around. No one in sight.

Charlie hurried toward the second bench and hid behind one of the Crepe Myrtles still in full bloom. A chubby man lumbered down the path. He was familiar. Charlie grinned. He stepped out from his hiding spot, silently walked up behind the man, and then yelled, "Hey!"

The heavy-set man stumbled and clutched his chest as a high squeak shot from his thick lips. "Holy, crap! Jesus and Mary!"

"Imagine seeing you here, Spanky."

"You 'bout gave me a coronary, McClung." Delicate white puffs rushed from his mouth with each heavy gasp.

Charlie saw beads of sweat profusely dotting Spanky's meaty face. "I've two questions. One, what are you doing here in Lyman County, Georgia? And two, why are you following me?"

Spanky leaned forward resting his hands on his thighs. "Give me a second while I catch my breath, will you, McClung? I'm not the young whippersnapper you are."

"Walk with me." Charlie slapped Spanky on the back a little harder than necessary, but doubted he felt it through the thick padding of fat.

Spanky fanned himself with his ever-present fedora. At one point in his life, Charlie had heard, Spanky was thought to be Frank Sinatra's long lost twin. Life had taken its toll on him, too much food and drink and advancing age.

"Whew, I need to start exercising or something." Spanky strolled with Charlie. "I didn't know you were here and I ain't following you, exactly."

"Is that right? Huh. Then tell me how we accidently crossed paths, again."

Spanky returned the fedora to his balding head. "Well, I ain't gonna lie. I'd heard the rumor you were living in Mayberry." He laughed.

"Yeah, the rumor is you're all Sheriff Andy Taylor now." Spanky snorted.

"Yeah, that's funny, a real rib-tickler." Charlie clamped his hand on Spanky's shoulder. "So tell me, why are you here?"

It was still too dark for Spanky to get a good look at McClung's face, but he could sense his nemesis's mood. "Yeah, well, I'll get straight to the point."

"I think that would be best."

Spanky's tongue ran around his mouth feeling for moisture. "I was supposed to meet a business associate." He felt a tighter grip on his shoulder.

Charlie was surprised. "Are you sure it wasn't Mitch Quinn?"

"Uh, I think you should stop digging your fingers into my shoulder. Kinda hurts, if you don't mind." Spanky rubbed his paroled shoulder. "Nope, it was definitely of the female persuasion."

"A woman was going to meet you in the woods, tonight. Really? Spanky, you expect me to believe you came all the way from Richmond to meet a woman?"

"Hand to heart. I'm telling you the truth."

The glowing lights surrounding The Primrose were beckoning and the sounds of life filtering outside was calming.

"Spanky, come inside with me and I'll introduce to you my wife."

"Don't tell me, you finally got married to …" Spanky repeatedly snapped his fingers. "Holly! Yeah, that's her name, Holly. So you finally married her."

"No."

41

Spanky stopped short. "No!" He beat his fingertips against his lined forehead. "Let me think. You've only been gone for what …" He tapped his forehead harder. "Six months?"

Charlie held open the door of the rear entrance of the kitchen. "Yeah, that's about right." He motioned Spanky to enter. "I finally found the one, so I married her."

Spanky arched his left eyebrow. "Huh, I gotta meet this one."

Charlie's mother stepped out of Joan's office, narrowly missing Spanky.

"Ah, son, who is this?"

Charlie kissed Ma's velvet-like cheek. "Just someone I ran into outside."

Ma eyed the stocky man. "Hmm, ya be lookin' like trouble ta me."

Spanky grunted.

"Ma, you have the gift of discernment. This is Myles Shumaker, affectionately known as Spanky. Spanky, this is my mother."

"Mister Shumaker." Ma extended her hand.

"Missus McClung." Spanky winced. The older woman's grip was stronger than her son's.

Charlie peered into Joan's office. Andrew was softly speaking with Joan. A dark blue bottle of sherry sat on the corner of the desk closest to Joan; her hand held a cordial with a splash of dark amber. He wondered how many Joan had had so far. Too many, and he wouldn't be able to interview her tonight.

"Spanky, come with me. Da is out there." Charlie pointed toward the double doors leading to the dining room.

A twinkle lit up Ma's eyes. She nodded knowingly as she spoke. "Aye, so ya be knowing me husband. So which sorta fellow are ya, a crook or a copper? I'm thinking ya be the first one."

Spanky looked at McClung. "So the whole family are a bunch of comedians." He rolled his eyes and pushed his way through the doors, not waiting for a reply.

Charlie grinned and threw his arm around Ma's shoulders, pulling her in close. "Ma, I hate to ask you but I promised my men biscuits and coffee."

Ma clicked her tongue and smirked. "How many do ya need?"

Charlie tugged his ear and grinned. "I'd say about two dozen."

"Poor child." Ma looked at Joan sitting silently. "I'll have her show me the whereabouts of things. It'll do her good to keep her mind busy."

He kissed his mother's cheek, inhaling the complex scent of Chanel No. 5. "Thanks, Ma."

He pushed through into the dining room. Da and Spanky had found each other by the dessert bar, neither one appeared to be thrilled with the chance encounter. Charlie observed that none of the guests appeared to be aware of what had happened. Candi was at the bar, more interested in Da and Spanky than the wine cooler in her hand.

"Spanky's been tellin' me ya found him a wanderin' the grounds. Is that right, son?"

Charlie stood next to Da, an older version of himself. "Yeah, claims he was supposed to be meeting a girl."

Da chuckled. "Aye, I can believe that. No lassie in their right mind would be meetin' him in the daylight. But what I don't understand, is why ya be comin' here for that."

Spanky picked up a plate, tossed a chocolate-dipped almond croissant on the plate, and then shoved half of another into his mouth. Flakes of pastry clung to his lips, fluttering into the air as he spoke. "You're quite the clowns. You two should call yourselves Bert and Squirt, join Saturday Night Live."

"Don't know nothing about that show." Da took one step away from Spanky.

"Well, what I want to know is, how did you avoid jail? Last time I saw you, you were being taken away in handcuffs." Charlie snagged a dark-chocolate covered strawberry, one of the few remaining, from the dessert bar.

Spanky alternated eating sweets and putting them on his plate. "Boss has a good lawyer."

Marian sidled-up next to Charlie. "My, another surprise guest. One of your friends?"

Spanky set down the empty plate. "Well, McClung, is this your wife?" He did a rapid inventory of Marian's features as he wiped his meaty hands, and then stared into her blue eyes.

Marian blushed.

"Marian, meet Myles Shumaker, not really what I'd call a friend. We have crossed paths during our lines of work."

She smiled, amused by her husband's wisecrack and extended her hand. "Nice to meet you, Mr. Shumaker. I'd love to chat. I'm sure I'd find your tales interesting."

"Call, me Spanky, Misses McClung." He lightly squeezed her delicate hand.

"Then, Spanky, you must call me Marian." She turned to Charlie. "Some of our friends would like to say goodbye," arching her left eyebrow as she said it.

Charlie understood. He needed to screen who had to stay and be interviewed. "Da, I leave him in your hands."

"Ah, nice." Da grabbed Spanky's elbow. "Ya stuffed yaself enough. Let's settle in at one of the tables."

Marian waited until she was sure Spanky would not overhear her comments. "Is that guy a crook? What's he doing? Did he kill Mitch?" She clung to Charlie's arm. "Please tell me he's a strong suspect. Please."

"Well, I can say he is a suspect, but strong? I'll know after he's questioned."

Marian smirked. "She's innocent. You have to know that."

Charlie turned her to face him, hands on both of her firm shoulders. "I will do the best I can to prove it, sweetie."

"I know," Marian whined softly and looked at her aching feet.

He tilted up her chin and lightly kissed her. "The sooner we get this place emptied, the sooner you can kick off those toe-crunchers."

She laughed and hugged him. "And the sooner we can catch the killer, right?"

"No, not we, but me and my guys." Charlie held his bride at arm's length. "You, I want to stay safe and out of trouble. Besides, you'll be busy tending to Joan."

Marian took Charlie's hand. "Fine. Let's go say goodbye to our friends." She glanced over her shoulder. Candi was still at the bar and Spanky was with Da. Marian wondered which one of them killed Mitch.

Chapter 6

Charlie looked around the empty dining room, well, almost empty. The wait staff were either cleaning up the dining room or in the kitchen. Candi chatted with the bartender as he shut down the bar. Da and Spanky were in the far back corner, entertaining each other with past offences, arrests, and stupid criminal stories.

The views from the windows were more distinct with the rising of the fall sun. Charlie was tired. All he wanted to do was go home and fall into bed with Marian. He put his hands on the small of his back and stretched.

Marian was now shoeless, having removed her heels as soon as the last of their friends walked out of the restaurant. Now, she was individually thanking the waiters and waitresses for their service and time, giving them each a small envelope containing a card and generous tip.

"Man, am I lucky." Charlie whispered to himself as he watched his wife walk around the room in her stocking feet. The musical sound of her laughter floated to his ears. He smiled. The sway of her hips as she walked made him wish they were home. Marian lightly touched each person's shoulder as she shook their hand. Charlie imagined her hand on his face, and shook his head. He needed to be thinking about solving Mitch's murder, not making love to his wife. Well, at least for this moment.

Marian walked toward Charlie. "I know that look on your face," she grinned shyly. "But that's going to have to wait." She wrapped her arms around his waist. "Joan has passed out in her office. Is it okay for me to take her home to our house?"

Charlie felt at peace in her embrace. "Sure, sweetie, go ahead and leave. Take Ma with you." He held Marian for a moment longer, gave her a hard squeeze, and then released her. "I can't question Joan now since she's drunk. I'll have to question her later in the day when she's good and sober. Normally, I'd take her in and put her in a cell to sleep it off, but I know she's not going anywhere under your watchful eye."

"Joan doesn't have any reason to run away. She's innocent." Marian looked around the room. "Are you going to take them all into the station for questioning?"

Charlie wanted to agree with his wife about Joan's innocence, but instead he answered her question. "I'll do the initial interviews here to determine who I need to take in." He gave her a quick peck on the lips. "Get going. I'll be home as soon as I can."

She headed toward the kitchen, stopped and turned, wiggled her fingers, and said with a wink, "Laters!"

Charlie laughed, knowing what she meant. That was one of the things he loved about his wife, her resiliency, to be able to deal with things as they come. He waved. "Laters, honey, laters."

Officer Wade Marshall, one of Charlie's newest additions to the force, stood guard upstairs at The Primrose where Charlie had segregated the potential suspects: Candi, Spanky, Andrew, and Heather. Luckily, the upstairs consisted of a large private banquet room and five more intimate rooms so each suspect had their own room. Charlie had quickly released the bartender and all employees that knew nothing of what Heather had revealed to Andrew concerning Mitch and Joan. They had been cautioned to stay in town because they may be questioned later.

"Officer Thayer, call for four cars to take our suspects to the station. Then report back here."

"What about Miss Delaney?"

"She's too drunk to interview; passed out in her office. We'll take care of her statement later today. I know we should take her in anyway, but I'm allowing her to go home under my wife's protection." Charlie paced in front of the bar, thinking what the next step should be. He could hear Candi complaining all the way from upstairs and he heard Heather crying because of her baby. Spanky was used to all of this; his complaint was lack of food. And Andrew, well, he seemed to be the calmest of them all. Curious.

"Yes, sir." The young officer turned on his heels.

Da stood beside his son to stop the pacing. "What would ya like for me to be doin'?"

"You should go be with Ma. Get some rest." Charlie slid his hand in his pants pocket. The car keys were missing, he quickly remembered Marian drove Joan and Ma to their house. "Aah, Marian has the car. I'll call a cab or better yet, I'll—"

"Don't be daft. Let me help. Are ya forgettin' I'm a copper?" Da held up his index finger, prohibiting Charlie to speak. "Yes, a retired one but once a copper always a copper."

Charlie rubbed the back of his head. He knew that to argue with Da was futile. "Sure Da, I can use your help. You can be with us during the interviews of those four." He pointed toward the ceiling. "The department had only two detectives, me and Harrison, who had been carted off to jail with Chief Miller. Officer Thayer will be assisting me with the interviews. I'd like to give him some experience. He's taken the detective's exam, still waiting on the results."

"Aye, he's a fine lad that boy is."

"Yep, I'm thankful Chief Miller hadn't had time to poison him." Charlie chuckled. "Plus, Sean had a plant in the department that took Thayer under his wing."

Da rubbed his graying chin stubble. "Ya brother did tell me about that after the fact. Top-notch agent posing as a country bumpkin copper, brilliant disguise I tell ya."

"Yeah, it's a definite advantage to have a brother in the FBI."

Officer Thayer returned. "The cars will be here shortly, sir."

"I need to lock up." Charlie jingled the key ring Marian had taken from Joan. "Officer Thayer, will you instruct Officer Marshall to bring everyone down and see they are taken to the precinct? And Thayer, I want you and Marshall to stay behind and wait for us out front. Da, come with me."

Charlie heard Candi complain she needed her beauty sleep all the way down the stairway and out the front door. She must have thought if she whined enough they'd let her go. Everyone else was silent as they trudged to the police cruisers.

After all the doors and windows were secured and lights turned off, Charlie set the alarm and locked the front door.

It was dawn. The air was chilly and the stars were still slightly visible, the new moon was nowhere to be seen. Charlie could hear the faint voices of his men standing guard in the forest. They sounded content. He guessed they were satisfied with Ma's biscuits, coffee, and a murder. Not that they should be happy about a murder, but it was a stranger, not someone they knew, and it did break up the monotony of a small town.

"Officer Marshall, I want you to patrol the perimeter of The Primrose. I'll send someone from first shift to relieve you." Charlie held out his hand. "Thank you for your hard work."

"Thank you, sir." The young officer had a trace of a smile.

"Officer Thayer, come with Da and me. I need to check the crime scene before you drive us to the office."

The officer followed beside Charlie as he hurried toward the woods. "I know your shift ends at seven, but I'd like you to be present for the interviews. If you need to go home, I'll understand."

"Yes, sir. I'd like the experience. No need for me to go home, not married yet, living with two roommates."

Charlie was glad to hear the eagerness in Officer Thayer's voice. "Good. Da will be joining us, too."

"I feel honored, Chief McClung, I mean … well, should I address you both as Chief McClung?"

Da laughed. "Aah, my days as chief are over, son. Just call me JP. It stands for John Patrick.

"Thank you sir. I mean JP." Officer Thayer reddened.

They were about to enter the forest when Charlie paused. A large shadow moved to the right of him. His hand gripped his revolver.

"Did you see that Thayer? Da?"

"No, sir, but I heard it."

"Aye, son, I got a glimpse of something."

The men drew their weapons and cautiously approached the area. The muffled sounds of retreating footfalls caused Charlie to stand down. "No point of chasing whatever it is."

"It could've been a deer, sir." Thayer replaced his weapon.

Da slid his gun into his ankle strap. "I agree. No point chasing after shadows."

"Let's hope. We'll have this area searched just to be sure." Charlie knew it wasn't a deer, but a human. He wondered if he was chasing after the wrong suspects, the four waiting for him at the precinct. Maybe the shadow was harmless. Maybe a nosey homeless person. Or maybe it was the killer or an accomplice. Too many variables to feel safe.

Charlie was thankful for the pot of freshly brewed coffee.

One of the officers he had sent to follow Marian home and then report to the crime scene, walked in carrying a platter covered in foil. "I'm sorry chief, but your wife threatened bodily harm if I didn't bring these to you right away."

"I understand. Let me apologize for her arm bending methods."

The officer set down the over-sized platter, removed the foil, and then quickly retreated.

Memories of the night he met Marian popped into his head when he saw a platter of cranberry-orange muffins sitting next to the coffee maker. The same kind of muffins she made that night. The night he found that special someone his granny said was waiting for him.

He picked up a muffin, inhaled its aroma, smiled, and thought what a lucky man he was. Marian must have made these as soon as she arrived home.

"Your wife is an excellent baker." Stewie, one of the administrators stood beside Charlie. "She's going to make me fat." The man patted his concave stomach.

Charlie looked at the painfully thin man. "Yeah, Stewie, I can almost see your shadow now." He poured a cup of coffee, peeled away the liner from a muffin, bit half of it, and then washed it down with coffee. "I see you made the coffee, Stewie. I think I just sprouted ten new hairs on my chest."

Stewie stared at McClung. After taking a gulp of the strong black coffee, he sighed, "Well, what can I say? I like my coffee like I like my women, strong." ·

Da chuckled. "Aye, son, I know what ya mean." He slapped Stewie's boney back, almost knocking him off his feet. Da grabbed Stewie's thin bicep. "Steady, now. I guess this coffee's given me a wee bit of strength."

The wisp of a man regained his posture. "Hmm, now I know where your son gets his sense of humor. And speaking of which, if you're going to get me up at the crack of dawn, tell me why, Chief."

"A man by the name of Mitch Quinn was found with his throat sliced open. See what you can dig up on the victim. Call my brother, Sean, if you have to. I want to know everything about the man. Everything."

Stewie removed a pad from his back pocket, clicked the pen from his shirt pocket, and scribbled notes. "Why are you so curious about the victim?"

"Joan Delaney was found standing over him with a bloody knife in her hand. Her chef's knife."

The pen froze, hovering over Stewie's pad. He glared at McClung. "Miss Delaney of The Primrose? That's not funny. Not the least bit amusing." Stewie watched McClung's face. "You're serious."

Charlie smirked. "I truly wish it was a sick joke."

"But …" Stewie cleared his throat. "I'll get right on it, sir."

Da watched the young man disappear down the hallway. "I can see our Joan is well loved by most everyone."

Charlie smiled at Da considering Joan as part of the family. And why not? Joan had traveled to Virginia on a moment's notice to be part of their wedding. The McClung clan had taken an instant shine to her.

"Yeah, Da, everyone loves that tiny little spitfire." Charlie rubbed the top of his head. "Especially, Marian." He sighed heavily. "I've got to prove she's innocent no matter what my own eyes saw."

"Ah, but ya didn't see her do it, now did ya?"

Charlie grinned at Da. "You're right. Looks can be deceiving." He squeezed Da's strong shoulder. "We've got suspects. Let's go."

His father rubbed his hands together. "Aye, to be back in the saddle, again. I'm with ya son. Let's go find the real murderer."

Chapter 7

"You believe me don't you? Tell me you do, please." Joan sobbed, her body trembled as Marian held her friend in her arms.

Marian rocked her best friend. "Don't be silly. You should know I do, sweetie." With tear-filled eyes, she watched her mother-in-law enter the guest bedroom with a pot of tea and a plate of crumpets and jam.

"Aye, I see our Joan is awake. Nothing like a cuppa tea to make things better."

Joan released Marian from her bear hug and collapsed on the mound of pillows behind her head. She ground the heels of her hands into her eyes, smudging her mascara. "God, this has to be a nightmare. This can't be real."

Marian pulled Joan's hands away from her eyes. "What are you trying to do, gouge out your eyes? Stop it!"

Joan looked like a cornered rabid raccoon.

Ma settled on the bed and crooned, "Oh, my sweet child," as she lovingly stroked Joan's hair, smoothing her rat's nest hair into place.

Seeing Ma working her calming charm on Joan, Marian poured out a cup of tea with a splash of cream. She set the cup on the nightstand, not wanting to disturb the moment.

Joan looked serene, nestled in Ma's embrace. Her head safely tucked under Ma's chin.

Marian didn't know whether to cry or smile. She had lost and gained so much in the past few years. Diane, her neighbor and surrogate little sister, was murdered. But in the midst of that sorrow, she had found Charlie, the love of her life, after mourning for her dead husband for almost twelve years. Her life felt complete, now she had Charlie and his family. Ma and Da easily filled the void her parents left when they died in a car crash eighteen years ago. Her only sibling Jeff lived in England, and now she had Charlie's brother and sisters and their families, all within driving distance of Virginia.

Joan, her truest and dearest friend, her crutch and lifeline for the past six years, may be ripped from her life for the murder of a man Marian had never heard Joan mention. What would she do without Joan?

Mounting anguish squeezed Marian's heart. She wiped away a small tear from the corner of her eye as she sandwiched Ma in between herself and Joan.

Ma kissed Marian's temple. "Ah, my love, everything will be all right. Our Charlie will make sure of that. Ya can count on it."

Joan and Marian threw their arms over Ma's ample bosom and hugged her tightly.

"I know Ma. I know he will." Marian closed her eyes and prayed.

Joan cried silently.

Ma let her girls rest on her shoulders. After a few moments when Joan's tears stopped, Ma kissed their foreheads. "Now then, let's have a cuppa, shall we?" She waited for the women to release their embrace and for Marian to stand before she stood next to her new daughter.

"I'll pour a fresh cup for you and Joan and I'll take this one." Marian pointed to the cup she had poured for Joan. "I like it at room temperature."

Ma patted Joan's wet cheek. "Here my flower. Drink this. Y'all see things in a different light after a cuppa and a crumpet buried under some jam."

Joan smiled weakly as she took the plate from Ma. The perfectly round bread with its buttery aroma took her mind away from the night's horror. "These look perfect. I haven't mastered crumpets." She took a bite. "Mmm, Ma, these are heavenly. You have to teach me how to make these. They'd be perfect for The Prim ..." Joan's lips trembled as reality reared its cruel head.

"No, no, no, child. We'll be having none of that while taking tea." Ma removed the plate tilting in Joan's hand, and then sat beside her with a steaming cup of tea. "Come on now, have a sip."

Joan stared at Ma's hand as tears dripped onto her lap.

Marian took the cup from Ma. She jumped on the other side of Joan. "Come on. You've nothing to worry about. Charlie's already questioning people. He's going to clear you."

"No, he can't. He can't." Joan's body shook the bed as she bawled.

Marian felt goosebumps march up her spine. She dreaded to ask what her best friend meant. "Joan, you didn't kill Mitch. I know you couldn't have. You just couldn't." She felt her eyes burn with a flood of tears.

Joan shook her head violently, and then squeezed her head between her hands. "Don't ask me to explain. Don't. Just don't"

Ma left the room.

Marian wondered why Ma disappeared, but then she returned with a couple of grayish brown capsules and a glass of water. Valerian root.

"Listen up, my girl." Ma pulled away Joan's hands from her face and held them.

Joan's chin rested on her chest, eyes closed.

"No, I'll have none of that. Look at me, child." Ma released Joan's hands and sat on the side of the bed.

Marian tucked a lock of Joan's hair behind her petite ear. "Come on, sweetie, you need to rest. No more talking. Okay?"

Joan leaned against Marian. "I'm so scared. I …" Her words were strangled by sobs.

"I'm here. Ma is here. We are going to take care of you. Charlie will find whoever caused this. There's nothing to worry about. Trust me." Marian felt Joan's head nod against her shoulder. "Okay. Now take these. They'll help you get some rest."

"Okay," Joan croaked, taking the capsules from Ma.

Marian watched as Joan swallowed the whole glass of water.

Ma handed a tissue to her, and she wiped Joan's moist nose. Marian eased her friend's body away from hers and onto the mound of pillows. "Now lay down and go to sleep. When you wake up, we'll have some honey orange oven-baked French toast, bacon, and coffee." Marian pulled the thick duvet over Joan's thin shoulders.

"I love your French toast," Joan whispered into the pillows.

"I know you do, sweetie." Marian turned on a cat-shaped nightlight next to the bedroom door. "I'm going to turn out the lights, but Ma and I will be just outside in the living room if you need anything. Okay?"

Joan yawned, "Uh-huh."

Marian pulled the door to, leaving it open an inch, so she could spy on Joan periodically without waking her.

Ma and Marian sat quietly eating crumpets and drinking tea. Flames roaring in the fireplace danced and weaved, casting shadows in the dim living room.

Ma broke the silence. "What do ya reckon she meant when she said, 'Charlie can't'?"

"I don't know but it's worrying me." Marian collapsed back onto the new leather sofa she and Charlie bought. She had her whole house remodeled with a revised floorplan and furniture after she had almost been killed inside her own home. Marian didn't want any reminder of that awful night. Thank goodness something good came out of it all. Charlie.

"What did ya and Charlie see in them woods?"

Marian rubbed her cold arms. "Joan standing in front of Mitch holding a bloody knife. She screamed it was her knife." She leaned forward and poured another cup of hot tea, and then cradled it between her hands hoping to overcome the chill.

Ma clicked her tongue. "Ah, the poor thing." She took a sip of tea, and then pursed her lips. "Ya know, I can't see Joan doing a thing like that." Ma nodded, "Our Charlie will uncover the truth. Ya can take that to the bank."

Marian smiled knowing Ma was right and felt the cloud of uncertainty float slowly away. The warmth of the fire wrapped around her like a reassuring hug. "You're right. I know he will."

Setting down her empty cup of tea, Ma rubbed her hands together, "I think I'll rest a bit before our husbands return." She stood slowly. "Ah, me bones are tired."

"That sounds like a good idea." Marian stood up and kissed Ma's soft cheek.

Ma put her arm around Marian's waist. "I love ya, child. Charlie found his granny's promise in ya that's for sure."

The two women walked toward Ma and Da's bedroom.

"Goodnight, my love." Ma held Marian's face between her warm hands and kissed her forehead. "I'll teach Joan and ya how to make crumpets. That'll keep her mind distracted." Ma patted her new daughter's shoulder. "Things will be all right."

"I love you, Ma," Marian hugged her. "Goodnight."

"Sweet dreams about crumpets for it's crumpets we make when we wake." Ma disappeared behind the bedroom door.

Marian looked in on Joan.

Joan lay on her back, left arm hooked over the top of her head. The sounds of heavy breathing and an occasional leg jerk let Marian know Joan was not having a peaceful sleep, but at least she was asleep.

Marian entered her bedroom without turning on the overhead light. The outside security lamps flooded the master bathroom with light which spilled into the bedroom. She followed the beam into the closet, undressed, and threw on a robe. The weight of the night's events had taken their toll. She yawned and hurried through her nightly rituals. Marian decided to follow her own advice and took two valerian root capsules. She knew she would be allowed only a few hours of sleep before Ma had her up and in the kitchen and she wanted those precious hours to be restful ones. She crawled into bed wishing Charlie was beside her and was sound asleep before she finished her prayers for her husband and Joan.

Chapter 8

"Who should be questioned first, Chief?" Officer Thayer waited for an order.

Charlie mulled over the title, Chief. He liked the sound of it even though he'd never considered being chief until the temporary title was bestowed upon him after Chief Perry Miller had been arrested. He'd been happy being a detective. Too many people to please and the politics that came with being chief made his skin crawl as if he were in a room full of snakes and no way out. But Da had been chief of Mercy City, his hometown, and seemed to enjoy it until he retired from the position.

Besides, Charlie had always worked in Richmond, the capitol of Virginia, quite larger than the whole of Lyman County which was similar in size to Mercy City. He'd have to speak with Da, get his opinion and of course, Marian's feelings about it would weigh heavily in his decision, that is if the job was even offered to him. Chief Charles Patrick McClung. It had a good ring, except for Charles. He'd have to insist on Charlie.

Da's hand on his shoulder brought Charlie back to the matter at hand. "We'll start with the young girl, the waitress, Heather Neely, so she can get home to her baby."

"Yes, sir. She happens to be waiting in interview room one."

Charlie motioned for Officer Thayer and Da to follow as he headed down the hallway. The sounds of their footfalls bounced off the linoleum floor, echoing off the concrete walls painted a light cream.

They entered the room on the other side of the two-way mirror to observe Heather before Charlie began the interview. She sat hunched over, staring at her hands. Charlie could tell by the movements of her arms that Heather was picking at her nails. She looked small and defeated. Her head snapped up and stared at the mirror as if she knew they were watching her. Hair that had escaped her ponytail drooped over her red, puffy round face. She'd been crying.

Charlie wondered how this tiny, pathetic, little girl could have a baby. Some boy must have made her promises of eternal love and devotion. He hoped the boy had done her right and married her. Charlie sighed. "Let's go find out if this girl knows anything."

When the three men entered the interview room, Heather stared at them, her dark eyes wide open, tears streamed down her freckled cheeks. She watched Da as he walked behind her to the corner of the room and spun around at the sound of the chairs scraping against the floor as Charlie and Officer Thayer sat down across from her.

Officer Thayer slid a thin manila folder toward Charlie.

Charlie opened it and read aloud. "Your name is Heather Morana Neeley?"

The young girl nodded.

"Please verbally answer the question, Miss Neely," Officer Thayer instructed her in a stern voice.

Heather flinched at his tone and softly replied, "Yes, sir, my name is Heather Neeley."

"And you're twenty-five years old?" Charlie thought she looked eighteen and wondered if the profile was wrong.

Her eyes darted from Charlie toward Officer Thayer, and then back to Charlie. "Yes, sir." Heather was still wearing a Primrose apron. She pulled up the bottom, blotted her eyes and wiped her dripping nose.

Charlie reached down under the table. Retrieving a box of tissues, he slid it toward Heather. The frightened girl reminded him of his niece, Mary Grace. Charlie wanted to be more sympathetic but he was a detective, not the girl's uncle.

"Thank you, sir." She grabbed a few and blew her nose.

"So you've been in Lyman County for a little over a month? And you live," Charlie squinted slightly, "with your boyfriend and ten-month old son at the extended stay inn."

"Yes, sir, well, I did until last week. He walked out on me and our son. I've been staying with my step-mother and Dad." Heather swallowed hard keeping her focus on Charlie's face. "I need them to watch my son while I work. I can't afford to pay a babysitter."

"Where do they live?" Charlie clicked his ink pen, ready to write down the address.

Heather sat in silence.

"The chief asked you a question young lady. Answer it."

65

Charlie laughed inside his head thinking Officer Thayer played a good bad-cop.

"They ain't got nothin' ta do with this." Heather straightened up her back, hands clutching the sides of the hard metal chair.

Charlie tilted his head to the side and wondered why her speech pattern and accent changed. "Where are you from originally?"

Heather rubbed her cheek and licked her dry lips. "Mississippi."

"Hmm, you don't have much of an accent, that is until just now."

"I worked hard getting rid of it. People would laugh at it, made me feel stupid."

Charlie looked at Da. "Would you mind getting Miss Neeley—," he stared at Heather. "Do you mind if I call you Heather?"

"No, sir."

"Thank you, Heather. I can see you're thirsty. Would you like something to drink?"

She smiled for the first time since she had been rounded up at The Primrose. "A Coca-Cola would be good."

Da left the room.

"So Heather, when did you leave Mississippi?

She relaxed back into the chair. "We lived with my mother until she died a couple of months ago, cancer." Heather pressed the used tissues to the corners of her eyes.

"I'm sorry for your loss." Charlie drummed his fingers on the wooden table. "Let me see if I have this right. You, your boyfriend, and son lived in Mississippi with your mother and after she died you moved in with your Father and step-mother."

Heather shook her head. "Not exactly. We lived with them for about a week, and then Bobby, my boyfriend got a job and we moved into the extended stay. I got the job at The Primrose a couple of weeks ago and that's when Bobby left, and I moved back with my father."

Da entered the room with a sweating can of Coke held with three fingers. He opened it before giving it to Heather.

"Thank you." She smiled at Da, and then took a deep drink. "Mmm, hits the spot." Heather then politely belched into the tissues, her cheeks pinked. "Excuse me."

Charlie nodded. "What's your boyfriend's full name?"

"Robert James Sorrows." She grunted, "Yah, the name suits him. Nothing but sorrows since I met him."

Charlie studied the girl's face. She did look distressed. He wondered if there was something else hiding behind her mascara-free eyes. Strange he thought, not a speck of make-up.

"Heather, where were you between midnight and one o'clock this morning?"

She looked puzzled. "At The Primrose."

"Yes, but exactly where at The Primrose, the kitchen, outside?" Charlie could see she was searching for an answer. "Surely, it's not that hard to answer."

Heather squirmed. "Well, don't tell Miss Delaney. I need this job."

"Just between us," Charlie waved his pen around the room that included Da and Officer Thayer. "None of us will tell."

She glanced at Da and smirked at Officer Thayer. "I stepped outside for a smoke. We're not supposed to smoke while we're at work, not even outside. Miss Delaney says cigarette smoke ruins the atmosphere." Heather hugged herself. "You're going to tell her, aren't you?"

"No, we won't." Charlie made a few notes. "You were outside. Did you see anyone?"

Heather pushed back a few strands of dark hair that had fallen close to her button nose. "I heard someone walking on the path that leads to the woods. I thought Miss Delaney was looking for me so I ran and hid behind some pine trees. That's when I saw that blonde woman talking to that fat man."

Charlie didn't need to ask who she meant. "Really? Did you hear anything they said?"

"No."

"How long did they talk? Did they act as if they knew each other?"

Heather shrugged, "I don't know. They didn't hug or anything like that and they only talked for a few seconds. I saw the fat man point toward the woods."

"Interesting." Charlie scribbled on his ever-present notepad and without looking up said, "Now, tell me where your father lives."

Heather took a drink of Coke, held the liquid in her mouth for a few seconds, considered Charlie's polite command, and then swallowed. "My father is a very private man. He wouldn't like for me to tell you where he lives."

"I see." Charlie leaned forward. "How are you getting home? Is your father picking you up? Going to call a taxi?"

She bit her bottom lip, then she leaned toward Charlie. "Are you arresting me?"

"No."

"Then I'd like to leave."

"Can you at least tell your father's name?"

"I said he's a very private man. May I leave now?"

Charlie shook his head and thought she wants to play hard ball. "Not right now. I've a few more questions, then you can go."

Heather slumped back and crossed her arms.

"You told Andrew that Miss Delaney was meeting Mitch Quinn. How did you know about that?"

"I overheard them while I was in the pantry."

Charlie scratched his chin. He wanted to go home and be with Marian. "Why don't you just tell me everything right now so you and I can get out of here? Not play hundred questions. All right?"

"I was in the pantry when Miss Delaney told everyone to leave the kitchen, but before I could get off the ladder and out the door, everyone was gone. Just Miss Delaney and that creepy guy was left. So I panicked, just froze. Then they argued about the past. That guy kept calling her Barbie and he wanted some money. A lot of money or he was going to tell you and your wife something about Miss Delaney's past so she agreed to meet him at midnight at the third bench." Heather uncrossed her arms, put her hands on the edge of the table and started to stand. "That's all. May I go now?"

"Sit down. The chief isn't finished. He'll tell you when you may leave."

Heather glared at Officer Thayer and plopped down, hard causing the metal chair to move. She grabbed the can of soda and gulped it down.

"I have just one more question. Did you see or hear Miss Delaney threaten the man?"

Heather shrugged. "Not really. I mean, I was standing right outside of the kitchen door at the waiter's station when that guy came out rubbing his neck. He looked at me, laughed, and then asked me for a paper napkin. He said and I quote, 'that crazy bitch tried to slit my throat'."

"Really? He laughed, wasn't upset? Was he bleeding?" Charlie was upset by this revelation.

"Yes, sir, he laughed. It didn't appear to bother him that his neck was bleeding." Heather drained the remaining Coke. "May I go now? I can find my own way home. No need to worry about that."

Charlie was curious about Heather's refusal to let them know where she was living, but that would be easy enough to find out. He looked at Officer Thayer and nodded.

The officer stood. "You can follow me, Miss Neeley. I'll escort you out of the building."

Heather stood, shoving the chair back, almost hitting the back wall.

Officer Thayer held open the door.

Smiling at Da and Charlie, she shoved passed Officer Thayer who rolled his eyes as he shook his head at the girl's lack of respect.

Charlie waited for the door to close completely, and then spoke to Da. "What do you think?"

"The lass is hiding something whether it's got anything to do with the murder, I just don't know." Da rubbed the back of his neck as he sat next to his son. "But I gotta tell ya, it doesn't sound good for our Joan."

Charlie braced his hands on his thighs. "No, Da, I'm afraid you're right." He stood and stretched both arms over his head. "Let's see what the other three have to say, and see what's found at the crime scene before we hang Joan."

"Aye, ya got that right. I need some of that sludge that Stewie fellow calls coffee."

Charlie pulled out a tissue and picked up the empty soda can. "Trust no one. Taking this for prints."

"Good thinkin' son."

The two men trudged down the hallway.

"Who are ya going to interview next?" Da asked as they entered the break room.

Charlie sat down the tissue-covered can, and then poured a half a cup of coffee, topping it off with half and half. He sipped the hot liquid as he looked around the empty room, wondering what his men were finding at the scene. "I'll speak with Candi, then Andrew, and leave Spanky for last."

Da grimaced as he swallowed the black coffee. "Aye, this stuff is brutal. I've always liked me coffee black, but this …" He poured a generous amount of creamer into the jet black liquid. Da laughed as he pulled out the stirrer from the coffee. "I'm surprised it didn't eat this."

Charlie almost snorted coffee through his nose. He sat down at one of the round tables and stared out the wall of glass. The courtyard was just beginning to peak through the darkness which meant it was getting close to seven o'clock in the morning. He didn't want to look at his watch and see how long he'd been away from his gentle bride.

"Why do you think Spanky is here?" Charlie stood and poured out the rest of the coffee, fished some change from his pocket, and then bought a diet Dr Pepper from the vending machine.

Da continued to sip the dark caramel colored coffee. "Whatever it is, it isn't good."

"Nope." Charlie picked up Heather's Coke can. "I need to get this into evidence before I begin to interview Candi which I know is going to be a rough one."

Da clamped his hand on his son's shoulder. "Aye, but ya love this job, don't ya son?"

Charlie smiled. "Yes, but not as much as I do Marian."

"Good answer. Keep thinkin' like that and y'all have a happy marriage just like ya Ma and I do." Da stood in thought. "Aye, I truly love ya Ma. Best thing that ever happened to me. Don't know what I'd do without that woman." He sniffed back a tear, and then took another sip of coffee. "I'm beginning to like this stuff."

Charlie grinned. "I know just how you feel, Da."

Chapter 9

"That girl is weird!" Officer Thayer announced when he met Charlie and Da standing outside of interview room two.

"Is that right?" Charlie held a folder containing Candi's profile.

Officer Thayer shook his head. "I watched Heather Neeley walk out the door, and then I followed her to see if someone was waiting on her. She disappeared around the corner of the building. I jogged over to see where she was heading and she took off down the road on foot at full speed toward downtown."

Charlie arched his eyebrows. "I guess she's in a hurry. Did you call one of the patrol cars to see if they could spot her?"

"Yes, sir."

"Good job. All we can do is wait." Charlie put his hand on the doorknob of the interview room. "Ready?"

"Ready." Officer Thayer followed Charlie with Da falling in behind.

When they entered the room, Candi's head rested on her arms lying on the table.

She jerked up her head. "Well, it's about time! Why am I even here? I need to get home and get some sleep. I've got to work tonight.

Where's Mitch?" Candi narrowed her eyes. "Is that why you drug me down here? Did he do something stupid and you think I've got something to do with it?"

"Well, Miss Evans—," Charlie was quickly cut short.

"It's Candi, with an i. What? Do you think I'm some old maid? Calling me Miss Evans, pffh!" She leaned back in disgust and mumbled, "Stupid cops," as she crossed her arms under her full breasts threatening to escape her low-cut dress.

Officer Thayer's cheeks burned bright pink and he cut his eyes toward Da standing in the corner.

Charlie had seen hundreds of women like her back in Richmond, and he could easily focus on her pale ice-blue eyes and garish eye makeup perfect for a darkened, smoke-filled room.

"All right, Candi, just answer the questions succinctly, and we'll be out of here in no time."

She rolled her eyes. "Whatever!"

"You're a stripper at the—,"

Candi slapped the table with the palm of her hand. "Artistic dancer!"

"In your words, 'whatever,' you work at Ken's Playhouse on Stewart Avenue. Is that correct?"

"Yes," Candi sighed wearily. "Why are you asking me all this crap again? One of your boys wrote it all down. You're holding it in your hand so just cut to the chase. All right! Be succinct yourself, how about it." She saw a touch of surprise on Charlie's face. "Yeah, I know what succinct means. I'm not ignorant."

"No one has accused you of that." Charlie watched Da hold back his laughter by biting his lips and scratching the top of his head.

"Well then, ask me your questions so I can get out of this joint."

Charlie poised his pen over the notepad. "How do you know Myles Shumaker or you may know him as Spanky?"

"I don't. Next question."

"I thought you wanted out of here, so stop playing dumb and tell me how you know Myles Shumaker. You were seen talking with him on the grounds of The Primrose."

Candi glared at Charlie. "You're talking about that fat guy?"

"Yes."

"I talk to a lot of men in my line of business, doesn't mean I know them."

Charlie exhaled heavily. "What did you and Spanky talk about?"

"I asked him if he'd seen a man walking around out here. He said he had and pointed toward the woods. That's all we said."

He scribbled on the pad thinking Heather had told the truth. "Did you see anyone else? Did you find Mitch?"

"No and no. I started down the path, then this sweet little, fluffy, gray kitty ran past me. I adore cats, so I chased after it. I got lost in the woods." Candi pouted. "I didn't catch the kitty and I cut the bottom of my foot." She removed her heels, stood, hiked up her dress, and then threw her foot on the table. "See."

The men could see the cut and her choice of underwear. None.

"You can sit back down. We all got an eye full." Even Charlie blushed this time. "How did you get a cut on your foot if you had shoes on?"

Candi sat down with a satisfied leer on her face. "You can't walk around on grass in these." She held up the stilettos.

"Have you ever seen Spanky before, maybe in Ken's Playhouse?"

She yawned. "Maybe, I don't know for sure. He kinda looks like the man Mitch was speaking with a couple of weeks ago. They were sitting in a corner. A real dark corner, you know. And don't ask me what they were talking about, because I was performing at the time. All I can say is Mitch was in a bad mood afterward."

"Hmm, interesting. You say that was a couple of weeks ago. What one, two, three weeks ago?"

Candi groaned. "Three weeks ago, I guess."

Charlie made a few more notes. "When did Mitch decide to come here, to The Primrose?"

"I don't know," Candi threw up her hands, "a few days after he spoke with that guy." She pulled on her bottom lip. "Mitch has been in a good mood since he told me."

Candi frowned. "You still haven't told me why I'm here."

Charlie cleared his throat. "You honestly don't know why you're here?"

She saw the serious look on Charlie's face and swallowed hard. "What has Mitch done? Do I need a lawyer?"

"I hate to inform you, Candi, but Mitch is dead. He's been murdered."

She blinked a few times as she processed Charlie's revelation. "Dead? But … I …wait a minute. You think I killed him?"

"That's what I'm trying to find out."

Candi shook her head violently. "No, I didn't. I didn't." She covered her face with both hands and took several deep breaths.

Charlie reached under the table for the tissue box, but dropped them on the table as Candi removed her hands. There were no tears.

"Look, I wasn't alone in those woods."

"But you said you didn't see anyone but Spanky." Charlie glanced at his notes. "Did I hear you wrong?"

She moistened her lips. "Listen, now, I know how bad this looks. Me, out in the woods. Mitch killed out there. But I wasn't the only one in them trees. No, I wasn't." Candi smiled weakly, "Besides, why would I want to kill my sugar daddy? He treated me fine, never once beat me or hurt me. Never. Gave me everything I wanted."

"I don't know." Charlie hunched up his shoulders. "Maybe jealous of Miss Delaney, his ex-wife?"

Candi laughed. "You think I'm jealous of some washed up old stripper? I mean, look at this." She stood and rubbed her hands down the sides of her breasts to her waist, and then around to her butt.

"Were you alone or not?"

Grinning like a cat licking milk off her whiskers, Candi eased down on her chair, and sang, "I know a secret you don't know."

Charlie had had enough. He was tired and wanted to be home with Marian, not investigating the death of some stripper's pimp. "Look, Candi with an i, I think you better remember this is a murder investigation. And right now, you're my number one suspect. So if you don't cooperate, I'll have Officer Thayer arrest you and throw you in jail. Is that what you want, Candi with an i?"

Officer Thayer stood, ready to handcuff her.

Candi's mouth dropped open and blinked rapidly. "No! I can't go to jail. I won't!"

"You will if you don't behave and answer my questions."

"Okay, okay, just give me a second." Candi sat straight, feet flat on the floor with her hands clutched on her lap. "This is what happened. Mitch owed some guys a lot of money. He said his ex-wife would give it to him because she used to be one of his best strippers and now she's a Miss High Society Hoity-Toity and wouldn't want her shiny little halo tarnished."

Charlie felt like someone had just punched him in the gut. Joan, a stripper? That's why she never spoke of her past. "Go on."

"When I saw her, his ex-wife, I was floored how beautiful she is. I mean, I'm a knock-out, but she's …," Candi was for a loss of words.

"So you were jealous."

Candi blurted, "Yes, but I didn't kill Mitch because I thought he might hook up with her. I mean we weren't exclusive. I mean in our business. Seriously." She rolled her eyes.

"But why did you follow Mitch?"

She dropped her stare down to her hands. "I guess, I just wanted to make sure their meeting was just about money. Not …," Candi looked up at Charlie. "I didn't want her to take my place as the star. I mean men come from all around just to see me perform. Do you know how humiliating it would be for some older woman to take my place?" Tears were clinging to the corner of her eyes.

Charlie felt a little bit sorry for Candi. The girl thought she had nothing going for her except her looks. He wondered what she'd do when they were gone.

"Let me get this straight. You followed Mitch to spy on him but not because you loved him. You thought Miss Delaney would take your spotlight on the stage."

"Yes," she whispered. Candi pulled her long silky hair over her shoulder and fanned it across her chest like a protective blanket.

"There wasn't a cat, was there?"

"No." She repeatedly combed her fingers through her hair.

"I didn't think so." Charlie paused. "But you said you weren't alone in the woods, yet you didn't see anyone. Explain that if you can."

"I heard someone out there walking around. I think there were at least two people out there besides me. There were shadows moving around in different places at the same time. I could see light filtering through the trees I think from the pathway, and I thought I heard Mitch talking to her."

Now Charlie was really depressed. First, that Joan was ever married to a creep like Mitch. Second, because she had taken off all of her clothes for money at one point in her life, and now Joan may have just been identified as the murderer of said creep. "You heard Miss Delaney, his ex-wife, talking to him?"

"I didn't say that. I said I heard him talking, never said I heard anyone else speak."

79

Charlie tugged his earlobe. "What makes you think he was talking to Miss Delaney?"

"Because Mitch said something like, it's about time. I wasn't close enough to hear everything clearly. The only reason I heard that bit was because he yelled it, then he lowered his voice, but I only heard him. Hell, it could've been that fat man with him for all I know."

"I'm curious. Why didn't you get closer? You went out there to spy on Mitch and Miss Delaney, right?"

Candi bobbed her head and finger-combed her hair faster. "Yeah, but I got spooked. Like I said, something or someone else was out there. I could hear twigs snapping all around me. It could've been a bear or wolf for all I knew. I didn't want to stick around to find out. So I high-tailed it back to the restaurant. As I was making my way back, that's when I heard the screaming and yelling. I had no clue Mitch had been killed."

"I'm curious. You knew Mitch and Miss Delaney were meeting in the woods. You heard the screaming. Then back at the restaurant, Mitch was nowhere to be seen. And you had to have seen the blood on Miss Delaney's hands and face. Where did you think the blood came from? Were you even concerned for Mitch?"

Candi looked like a doe caught in the headlights. "Yeah, I did but I just thought maybe Mitch decided to get even for what she'd done." Her fingertips brushed her neck. "You know stabbing him in the neck. I thought maybe he had given her some of her own medicine." She searched Charlie's face for reassurance he believed her.

Charlie sat stone-faced.

Candi threw her hair back over her shoulder. "I'm telling you the truth. That's what I thought happened. I thought you were going to make me share the blame for him hurting her. Honest!" She cried, "I want to go home, now. I didn't have nothing to do with what happened out there in the woods. Please, let me go home."

Charlie squeezed the tight muscles in the back of his neck. "Fine. You can go, but don't leave town. You're still part of this murder investigation."

"Thank you, I understand." Candi leaned over to buckle the thin straps around her ankles. Her breasts jiggled like Jell-O, and threaten to tumble free from her dress. "Can someone call me a taxi? Mitch was my ride. And can you hand me a tissue?"

Charlie slid the box of tissues across the table, amazed how quickly she recovered as she tapped the corners of her eyes with a tissue.

"Officer Thayer, escort her out and call a cab for her." Charlie pulled out his wallet. "Here." He gave Candi his card. "If you think of anything, anything at all, give me a call."

"I will."

Charlie handed a twenty dollar bill to Officer Thayer. "For the taxi."

Candi looked at Charlie. "I guess not all cops are jerks." She blew him a kiss as she left the room.

Chapter 10

"Stewie, see what you can dig up on Candace Marie Evans, better known as Candi with an i and Heather Morana Neely." Charlie set two dossiers on the thin man's desk.

He picked up a thicker manila folder and opened it to the first page. "Hmm, Candi should be a breeze." Stewie spoke to Charlie as he flipped through the pages, "But if I hit a roadblock, should I call your FBI connection?"

"Sure, I'll call my brother to give him a heads up. And you know to identify yourself with your full name. Sean's not keen with nicknames. Don't ask why."

"Yes, sir. Is there anyone else I need to be scrutinizing?"

Charlie grinned, "You read my mind. Mitchel Daniel Quinn. He should have an interesting background. There's a connection between him and Candi. Also, Myles Ely Shumaker and Andrew Aaron Johnston."

"So in other words, everyone you hauled in tonight."

"Bingo! I still have Myles and Andrew to interview; I'll give you their files when I'm done. And then I'm going to run home to check on Joan. Marian's keeping a close eye on her." Charlie leaned his back against the wall, and then stared at the ceiling. "Man, I hope I can prove Joan didn't do this. That's going to be one tough interview." He pushed away from the wall. "And I hope within the next few days, we can prove Joan's innocence."

"Roger that, chief." Stewie clicked away on the keyboard. "I'll get this done and in your hands today." He whipped around in his chair to face Charlie. "Can't guarantee a time, but it'll be done today," and then he swung around to face his monitor.

"You're the best, Stewie."

Without turning around, Stewie replied, "Yes, sir, but in all fairness, Jenny is my right-hand. We're a team. We are the best."

Charlie thought of Jenny Stacks, the other professional assistant. She would be thrilled to know how her partner felt about her. "You're right. I couldn't do this job without the two of you."

He left Stewie and Jenny's office but didn't make it too far down the hallway before a thought popped into his head. Charlie returned to their office. "Hey, one more thing; I sent a Coke can to the lab with Heather's fingerprints on it. As soon as you get the results, call me. I don't care where I am or what time it is. Call me."

Stewie twirled around, gave Charlie a quick salute, and then turned back to face the monitor.

Charlie smiled, and then continued down the hallway to interview Andrew.

Da and Officer Thayer chatted outside of interview room one as Charlie approached. He thought Da looked tired compared to the young officer's giddy up and go expression. Charlie wished his father would go home and get some much needed rest, but he knew this was where Da wanted to be. And that made Charlie feel good inside, knowing his father was happy to be by his side.

Charlie gripped Da's firm shoulder and looked at Officer Thayer's eager face. "Ready, guys?"

The two men nodded silently as Officer Thayer handed his boss a thin folder holding Andrew's initial statement.

Charlie led the way into the small, brightly lit room.

Andrew sat with his chin resting close to his wide chest, both hands lay on his meaty thighs, and a soft snore could be heard coming from his open mouth.

Da, with one eyebrow cocked, looked at Charlie as he pointed his head to the sleeping young man.

Charlie understood what Da was saying. The boy was either a heavy sleeper or an ex-con.

Da stomped loudly on his way to the corner of the room closest to Andrew.

The young man didn't stir.

Officer Thayer and Charlie plopped down on their chairs, and then scooted them closer to the table, creating a loud scraping echo in the room.

Still, Andrew didn't move.

Charlie whispered, "Andrew."

His eyes popped open as he jerked awake. Andrew scanned the room. "Jesus! You guys scared the …" He thought better than to finish his sentence as he ran his fingers through his thick sandy-blonde hair. "I must've dozed off for a second."

"Yeah, I guess so from the looks of it." Charlie flipped open the folder. "Tell me, Andrew, what were you in for?"

The waiter licked his lips and feigned confusion. He leaned forward slightly, "I'm sorry, what?"

"You know what I'm talking about. Which crime did you commit?" Charlie watched Andrew think about his answer.

Andrew held his breath as he decided whether to tell the truth or not. He exhaled loudly and his shoulders sagged. "Theft of a non-commercial vehicle valued more than five-thousand dollars but less than twenty-five-thousand dollars."

"Hmm, what did you steal?"

The young man grinned. "Top of the line, fully loaded, 1977 Cadillac Seville, worth more than thirteen grand."

"How did you get caught?"

"Landlady ratted on me before I could fence it."

Charlie nodded. "Didn't always pay your rent on time?"

"No, sir." Andrew chuckled. "I thought I'd get away with it too. I parked in the dead of night, out of sight, but that old crow saw me. For the life of me, I don't know how."

"So, why did you steal it?"

He grinned and shook his head. "That's the funny thing about it." Andrew leaned forward and rested his forearms on the table. "I stole it to pay my past due rent so the old crow wouldn't have me evicted."

"How long were you in for?"

"I was sentenced to seven years, but served less than five. I got out six months ago on good behavior."

Charlie glanced at the open folder. "Says here, you've worked for Miss Delaney for three months."

"That's right. She's the only person who'd give me a chance." Andrew sat straight. "She's been real good to me."

Charlie watched the muscles work in Andrew's jaws, as if he were fighting to keep words or feelings from escaping. "You care for Miss Delaney, don't you?"

He nodded. "She couldn't have killed that man. Miss Delaney is a decent woman. I don't believe she'd do a thing like that."

"You mean slit a man's throat?"

Andrew recoiled. "What?" He sat in disbelief for a second. "No! Never! It couldn't have been her. It had to be someone else."

"Like who? You?"

"Christ, no! I'm a bad car thief, not a murderer, and neither is she. No way!"

Charlie tapped his thumb on the edge of the table. "You've only known Miss Delaney for three months, right?"

"Yes."

"So why do you think she's not capable of murder?"

Andrew blushed. "Now, don't take this the wrong way. Okay?"

Charlie shook his head and shrugged. "Depends on what you say, son."

He scratched the light stubble on his cheek as he considered his words. "It's like this, you see, I care about her, a lot. So, uhm, I've been watching her, sorta."

"Sorta?" Charlie held up his hands. "Can you sorta explain what you mean, watching her?"

"You know, around the restaurant. How she treats customers and us, the staff I mean. She never yells at us, even if we break stuff, expensive stuff."

Charlie tugged his earlobe. "Do you break a lot of stuff?"

"No, but," Andrew looked frustrated. "Like the other day, Heather dropped a tray of crystal flutes. Did Miss Delaney get upset? No, her only concern was for Heather. If she was cut or hurt. Miss Delaney even helped Heather clean up the broken glass."

Charlie made a few notes. "And do you watch her in any other ways?"

"Yeah, when she goes out into the garden and forest, but only to make sure Miss Delaney is safe. Obviously, there are some pretty bad people around here."

"Obviously. What does Miss Delaney do out there in the woods?"

Andrew smiled. "She makes sure the wild animals are cared for, like throwing out dried corn and peanuts for the squirrels and deer. She fills up the bird feeders and makes sure the hummingbirds have fresh sugar water."

"And doing things like that doesn't make her a murderer in your eyes?"

Bafflement clouded Andrew's face. "Well, no. Someone with a kind and tender heart like that couldn't kill anyone. Honestly, how cold-blooded do you think she is?"

Unreasonable guilt formed a lump in Charlie's throat. "I don't think she did it, but someone did and I need you to help me find out. Did Heather tell you about the meeting in the woods because she knew you cared for Miss Delaney? How did she find out that you were in love with Miss Delaney?

Andrew's cheeks burned red. "Heather had been watching me watching Miss Delaney."

"Interesting." Charlie shifted in his chair. "Could it be possible she was watching Miss Delaney and happened to notice you following her?"

Andrew rubbed behind his ear. "I guess that's possible."

Charlie cleared his throat. "Okay, let's get back to last night. Tell me everything you remember."

"Like I said before," he pointed to the folder lying on the table in front of Charlie, "everything was normal up until porn star guy comes into the kitchen and Miss Delaney orders everyone out."

Officer Thayer snickered, "Porn star," and then quickly recovered. "Sorry, sir."

Andrew coughed. "May I have some water?"

Da took his cue and left the room.

Charlie waited for Andrew to continue.

"I went back into the kitchen. I didn't like the looks of that creep, and thought Miss Delancy might need me. Instead of needing me, she asked me to go check on you and your wife. So I did as she asked. I left."

Da entered the room with a cup of ice water.

Andrew drank half of the cup, and then started up where he had left off. "After the guy left the kitchen, Heather pulled me into the wait staff station. She said Miss Delaney had gotten into an argument with that guy, and then she pointed toward the porn star guy. Then she tells me Miss Delaney was so mad at the guy, she tried to cut his throat."

"Did you wonder how Heather knew all of this since everyone was ordered to leave the kitchen?"

"Yeah, so I asked her how she could know all that. Heather then tells some story about being in the pantry afraid to leave because she might be accused of stealing canned milk for her baby."

Charlie waved his hand for Andrew to stop talking. "Wait a minute. Was Heather stealing from The Primrose?"

"I don't know. I didn't even know she had a baby, but then again she's only been on the job for a few weeks and she keeps to herself."

While jotting down a few notes, Charlie wondered why Heather left that part out. Surely, she didn't think he'd arrest her for stealing. "Okay, what did Heather say next?"

The young waiter finished off the water. "She said Miss Delaney and that guy were going to meet in the woods at the third bench after midnight. And she was scared that guy might hurt Miss Delaney because she tried to cut his throat."

"Did she tell you after midnight or at midnight?"

"Definitely after midnight because that's when Miss Delaney left, a few minutes after midnight."

"And you would know when she left because you were watching her."

Andrew nodded sheepishly.

Charlie jotted down a few more notes. "Was Miss Delaney carrying a knife or a bag or a purse when she left to meet Mitch?"

"No, none of those things."

"Interesting."

"Chief McClung, may I ask you a question?"

Charlie considered Andrew's request. "Sure."

"That guy called her Barbie. Why?"

Officer Thayer interrupted. "That's none of your concern."

"Okay, I see, none of my business. One more question then, see if I can get an answer to this one. The guy also asked Miss Delaney how many times she'd been married. Please tell me she wasn't married to him."

Charlie exhaled deeply. "I can't be certain but Mitch Quinn told me he used to be married to her. We haven't verified it yet. This case is still fluid."

Andrew was clearly upset and held the cup of melting ice to his throat and forehead. "It's getting hot in here."

"I have a few more questions, then you can go home. First, how did you get outside? Did you use the kitchen's backdoor?"

"Yes."

Charlie decided to just ask the young man to spit it all out. He was tired and wanted to go home to be with Marian even if it would be for just a few hours.

"Andrew, just tell us everything you remember. What you saw when you left The Primrose. If you can do that, we can all get out of here sooner rather than later. All right?"

The stocky young waiter rubbed his hands on the sweating cup, then ran his wet hands on the back of his neck. "I waited a few minutes before I followed Miss Delaney. I didn't want her to spot me. When I did leave out of the backdoor, I went down the path toward the third bench in the forest. I made it to the first bench without seeing anyone, and that's when I heard the screaming. I took off running and I could hear someone running down the path in front of me. I guess it was you and your wife now that I think about it.

"Yes, that was us."

Andrew shook his finger. "Yeah, but there was someone or something else in the woods. Stuff was snapping, popping, and breaking all around me." He hunched up shoulders. "Maybe it was just a bunch of deer. I don't know. I just wanted to find Miss Delaney to make sure she was all right."

Charlie scribbled on his notepad, *description of sounds in the forest similar to Candi Evans. Andrew saw no one*. "What did you see when you came upon Miss Delaney and my wife?"

"Your wife pointing a gun at me. That was the first thing I saw. Scared the hell out of me!"

The three cops laughed, Da the hardest.

"Well, you're lucky she didn't shoot you or we wouldn't be talking right now. My Marian's a fine shot." Charlie chuckled, again, as he envisioned Andrew with his hands in the air. "Where was Miss Delaney?"

"She was hiding behind your wife." Andrew grinned. "I had to convince them I wasn't the bad guy."

"Tell me what else you saw or heard."

"That guy was sitting on the bench. He looked like he was sleeping. Your wife wouldn't let me near him. Said he was dead and the area was a crime scene."

Charlie was impressed with his wife. "Anything else?"

"I heard you walking back out of the woods and that's about it. My main concern was Miss Delaney."

Charlie's head began to throb. He needed some rest, but it would have to wait. "I think that's all for now." Charlie slid his card across the table. "If you think of anything, call me. And you know don't —."

Andrew finished his sentence, "Don't leave town. Yeah, I know. Trust me. I won't walk out on Miss Delaney."

Chapter 11

Marian jerked awake. She flung her right arm over the right side of the bed. Empty and cold. Her mind was cloudy. Where's Charlie? Then she remembered. She threw the covers back, and then sat on the edge of the bed, her feet dangled, not touching the floor. After she and Charlie married, his bed replaced hers. Sliding off the bed, she looked at the clock sitting on the nightstand, 7:54.

The aroma of coffee filled her nostrils. Ma must be in the kitchen. Marian rushed into the master bathroom, ran a brush through her thick wavy hair, slipped on a pair of fuzzy house shoes, and threw on a warm robe not worrying about changing out of her flannel pajamas.

She opened the bedroom door, and tipped-toed over to the guest bedroom occupied by Joan. Peeking in, Marian saw Joan laying on her side, sound asleep. Good.

Marian walked into the great room, now after extensive renovations, completely open to the kitchen. Ma sat on a barstool and studied a homemade recipe book, unware Marian was watching her.

"Good morning, Ma."

Ma smiled at the sight of her son's lovely bride. "Morning, love. I was reading this binder you have filled with tried and true recipes."

Marian kissed her mother-in-law's soft cheek. "Did you see the recipe for the Honey Orange French toast I promised Joan?"

"Aye, I did indeed." Ma tilted her head toward the granite counter next to the wall oven. All of the ingredients for it were laid out.

Marian bear-hugged Ma from behind. "Thank you." She kissed Ma's other cheek. "I should get cracking. I'd like to jump in the shower before Charlie and Da get home." She looked at Ma's coiffed flaming red hair and makeup perfectly applied. It was no wonder Da adored her. Ma was elegant, charming, yet motherly at the same time.

Ma hopped off the tall stool and adjusted the wide black belt that cinched the emerald green tunic hanging mid-thigh over a pair of black stirrup pants. "Go on now. I think I can make ya proud." She cracked eggs into a wide, shallow bowl.

Marian laughed and tried to take the whisk from Ma's hand. "I wasn't hinting for you to cook breakfast."

Her mother-in-law was fast and grabbed Marian's wrist. "Shush, get yourself in the shower, love."

Marian scampered to the master bathroom. She flipped on the exhaust fan, turned on the shower, and then undressed. Stepping into the steam, she sighed. The hot water felt good on her neck and shoulders tight from stress. Marian wanted to linger but knew, or rather hoped, that Charlie would be home soon. So instead, she flew through her morning routine.

As she dressed, Marian could smell the sweet, orange aroma of the French toast drifting out of the kitchen and into her bedroom. Her heart quickened when she heard Ma speaking to someone, and then she heard Joan's unmistakable Carol Burnett laugh. Marian was thrilled to hear Joan's laughter, but had hoped it was Charlie that Ma had spoken to. She finished dressing, and then joined Ma and Joan in the kitchen.

Joan sat at the breakfast bar with a mug in her hands, and her elbows resting on the countertop. Marian noticed Joan had smoothed down her hair and cleaned up her eye makeup, and wore a pink terrycloth robe.

"What are you two laughing about?" Marian jumped up on a barstool next to her best friend in the entire world.

Joan set her mug down, and then hugged Marian. "You have the best mother-in-law ever."

Marian heard a twinge of sadness in Joan's voice. She didn't know much about her friend's past, but evidently there wasn't a kind mother-in-law in Joan's history.

"I know. I'm one lucky woman." Marian looked at Ma as she leaned back against the countertop. She saw a warm, happy glow on Ma's face, and then it melted with sadness.

Joan was crying.

Marian hopped off the barstool, wrapped her arms around Joan, and slowly rocked her. "Shhh." Marian felt Ma's warm embrace around the both of them.

"Ah, now my pretty little loves. Ya both are my darling daughters. Don't ya know that? And I'll not be letting nothing bad to happen to neither one of ya. Understand?"

Joan's body shook with each anguished sob.

Ma kissed Marian's cheek and whispered into her ear, "I think the oven needs to be checked," and then released Marian.

As soon as Marian stepped away from Joan, Ma turned Joan's barstool, and then hopped up beside her. Now facing Joan, Ma cradled Joan's wet face in her soft, strong hands. "Listen, love, my Charlie and his Da will get to the bottom of this mess, and you'll not be in it no more."

Joan continued to cry as she avoided Ma's bright blue eyes.

"Come on, now, child. Look at me." Ma's voice soothing.

She hesitantly shifted her gaze from the floor to Ma's loving face. "Oh, Ma, you don't know what I've done." Joan's tears spilled over Ma's hands.

Marian dropped the hot pan of French toast, luckily, on the counter, stared at her best friend, and wondered what Joan meant by her words. Surely, they weren't about last night.

"Well, now love, I know one thing and that's ya no murderer." Ma released Joan's face. "Marian, my flower, toss me one of those dish towels." She pointed toward a hand-carved wooden bowl with rolled towels neatly stacked.

Marian obeyed, snatched off the top one, and then hurried over to Ma.

Taking the towel, Ma gently blotted Joan's face, eyes, and nose.

Joan held Ma's wrists. "If you knew the things I've done," she stared at the floor and released her grip, "you wouldn't want me for your daughter or friend."

Marian rushed to her dejected friend and slid her arm across Joan's shoulders. "There's nothing that could make me stop loving you."

Just above a whisper, Joan replied, "But you don't know the sins of my youth. They're horrible."

Ma clicked her tongue. "Tis the past, my sweet. Listen to ya sister. Nothing can break our bond, past nor present."

"That's right. You're stuck with us, Joan."

"But—,"

Ma touched Joan's lips with her finger. "No, we'll not be having none of that."

"But I want you to—,"

"Shush! I'm no priest, neither is our Marian. We'll be hearing no confessions. Do ya understand, my darling?"

Joan nodded weakly.

Ma slid off the barstool. "Good." She clutched Marian and Joan's hands. "We've a perfectly good batch of Honey Orange French toast waiting to be eaten. And then I'll be teaching my two lovely daughters how to make crumpets."

Chapter 12

Charlie hung up the phone, then looked at his watch, 8:01. He wondered when this morning would end. Chuckling to himself, he softly said, "Noon." He counted himself lucky that Sean was already in his office with the FBI. His brother instructed him to tell Stewie that if he wasn't available, to speak with his assistant, Edward, who would help Stewie with whatever information he needed.

Charlie rubbed the back of his neck and the top of his shoulders, wishing it was Marian's hands massaging his knotted muscles. He reached for the phone to call her, but decided against it. The sooner he questioned Spanky, the sooner he could go home and kiss his wife, instead of hearing her voice and aching to be with her. Besides, he didn't want to wake her.

He looked out the glass wall of the office toward the officers' cubicles. A few of his men sat at their desks filing reports. Most of the officers, on-duty and off-duty, were still at the scene of the crime. He'd have to wait until the criminal investigation team was finished and for Jack to finish the autopsy before he could get the complete picture of what happened out in the woods.

He pushed away from the large oak desk that used to belong to his old chief, Perry Miller, and then exited his temporary office. Heading toward the stairwell, he passed the unsolved-case whiteboard. Just one listed. *Mitchel Daniel Quinn – Murder.*

Charlie jogged down the stairs and made his way to interview Spanky. There stood Da and Officer Thayer patiently waiting for his arrival.

"All right, let's get this done so we can get home." Charlie entered the small room. The other two men took their places.

Spanky still wore his fedora and stared stone-faced at Charlie. "What? You don't think I have a life? Keeping me waiting like this. I got things to do and people to see. Let's get this over with so I can be about my business, shall we?" He removed his hat and rubbed his bald head.

Charlie ground his teeth and inhaled to control his urge to punch the fat man's nose. He was tired, hungry, missed his wife, and had a very good friend who was the number one suspect in the murder of a two-bit hustler, not that it mattered what Mitch was. Murder was murder. Charlie pushed himself back into the hard wooden chair, sat at attention, and then glared at the large man sitting across from him.

"I'm disappointed in you, Spanky. You should know by now, us McClungs don't tolerate disrespect."

Da spoke for the first time. He took a few steps and spoke into the suspect's ear. "Myles, ya best behave."

Spanky's demeanor changed. He smiled and snorted, "Yes, sir."

Charlie cleared his throat. "Look, you want to leave. Officer Thayer wants to leave." He circled his hand around the room. "We all want to leave. You know how this works, so save us some time, and spill your guts. If I have questions, I'll interrupt you. Deal?"

Spanky considered the proposition, shrugged, replaced his hat on his sweaty head, and then spoke. "Like I told you guys before, I came down here to meet with a girl, uh work related thing. I don't know nothing about no murder."

"Who's the girl?"

"Well, I'm not at liberty to say."

Charlie leaned forward.

Spanky threw up his hands. "Now don't go all bad cop on me. It's just I don't see the correlation of my business with all of this."

"Answer the chief's question." Officer Thayer's hand rested on his baton.

"Like I said, I was supposed to meet this girl about a business opportunity in Virginia, working at one of the boss's clubs."

Charlie grinned. He was beginning to see a different picture from the one Candi had painted. "So if you were here to meet with Candi, why were you talking to Mitch a few weeks back at Ken's?" Charlie saw Spanky's left eye twitch. "Yeah, she told me she thought she saw you talking to Mitch. Said he was in a bad mood afterward because he owed you money."

The overweight man's forehead was beaded with sweat as he held his breath. Spanky exhaled slowly. He took off the black fedora, and then fanned himself. "Is it getting hot in here?" He looked to each of the men's faces. "You guys hot? Could I get some water?" He hooked his finger on his collar above his tie and pulled. The top button of his shirt threaten to pop off.

Da left the room to get the nervous man some water.

"I can explain that. Uh, it's like this. Mitch was behind on a small loan. Yeah, I guess that was the real reason I was in town."

Charlie smirked. "You guess?"

Sweat trickled down Spanky's temples. "Yeah, that's why I came to Georgia, initially. The loan that is. Then, I saw Candi." He leered. "Boy, can that girl move."

Spanky yanked out a few tissues from the battered box of tissues on the table. As he blotted his face, he continued to speak. "Like I was saying, Mitch owed the boss forty-five thousand dollars plus interest. And after I saw Candi doing her stuff up on the stage, I thought she'd be a valuable asset for the boss."

"Did Mitch know you were going to make an offer to Candi? Better yet, did Candi even know?"

Da entered the room with two cups of water, and set them in the middle of the table.

Spanky held up his meaty hand. "I'll answer that after I wet my whistle." He downed one of the cups. "Mm, most refreshing." He wiped his mouth with a tissue, and then sighed. "No, Mitch didn't know. But Candi knew. I went back stage that night. We talked. She said she'd think about it."

"All right, so how did the three of you end up at The Primrose?"

Spanky tapped the side of his rosy nose. "Ah, good question. Mitch called a few days after our business meeting, said he'd have the money to me by the eighteenth which you know is Monday."

"Yeah, go on." Charlie scribbled a few notes on his pad.

"Then the next thing I know, Candi calls, wants to meet me. Long story short, that's how we three ended up at The Primrose." Spanky reached for the second cup of water.

Charlie scratched his head. "The two of you arranged to kill Mitch?"

Spanky's hand jerked as he brought the cup to his full lips; water spilled down his chin and chest. "No! God, no!" He set the empty cup on the table, and then blotted the water from his clothes. "I had nothing to do with that. Honest."

Da laughed. "Ah, Spanky, ya don't have a honest bone inside ya."

The hefty man craned his neck around toward Da. "Yeah, well, that may be but I didn't kill Mitch nor arrange to have him killed. Kinda useless to me dead. I wanted that money."

Charlie looked at Da and Officer Thayer. "The man makes a good point. But like you said earlier, Candi is a valuable asset. I don't see Mitch letting her go. Maybe that was the only way you two could arrange that. You know, with Mitch out of the picture, she'd be free to dance for whomever."

Spanky licked his thick lips. "Now wait a minute. You ain't gonna pin no murder on me. I may be the criminal kind, but I ain't no murderer. No, sir, you're not pinning that on me!" He crossed his wrists over his pregnant-shaped belly as he shook his head.

Charlie felt inclined to believe him. "Then make your short story longer. Give me the details of your meeting."

"Gladly. Mitch called, asked me to be at the club on the eighteenth and he'd have all the money for me. Then two days after Mitch called, Candi rings me. Said she thought about my proposition and wanted to discuss the details. Candi asked me to meet her at The Primrose on the sixteenth after midnight. She told me to wait for her outside of the restaurant."

As he tapped his pen on the notepad, Charlie thought about Spanky's last comment. "Now let me get this straight. Mitch was going to give you the money at his club. No mention of how he was getting the money?"

"Nope. I didn't care how he got it, just that he had it all."

"And Candi called you and made the arrangements to meet at The Primrose after midnight. Did she say why she wanted to meet there?"

Spanky seemed to relax. "Yeah, she said she had the night off. That Mitch was going to meet his rich ex-wife at some fancy, upscale joint and he was taking her with him. Said it was her only chance to meet me without Mitch getting suspicious."

Charlie stared at the corner of the ceiling. After a few seconds, he crossed his arms and leaned comfortably back against his chair. "So, I guess it was quite a shock to see Mitch come out of the restaurant before Candi?"

"Yeah, 'bout had a coronary. A pimp doesn't like you messing around with his inventory." Spanky giggled nervously. "But I could tell by his walk he was on a mission to meet someone. Then I thought maybe it was Candi he was going to meet for a little *somethin'* in the woods because a few minutes later, she comes out barefooted, carrying her shoes. I catch her attention. She sees me and screeches, 'Did you see Mitch?' I asked her what was going on and if we were still going to discuss business. All she says is, 'which way did he go'?"

Charlie smiled. "More interested in Mitch than you. How did that make you feel?"

"Humph! The girl needs to learn some respect. I take time to meet her, then she blows me off to chase after her pimp." Spanky rolled his eyes. "She ran across the yard, then headed for the trees."

"Did you follow her?"

Spanky leaned forward, his hands resting on his thighs for support. "Yeah, but I didn't get far before I saw a pretty little blonde marching down the path." He shook his thick index finger at Charlie. "Now that one looked pretty pissed."

Charlie knew that pretty little blonde was Joan. "Yeah?"

"Yeah, if I were you, I'd be questioning her, not innocent people like myself. That one looked to me as if she had murder in mind."

"Thank you for your advice," Charlie sneered.

Spanky shrugged as he threw up his hands.

"What happened after that?"

"I heard a scream come from the forest, and then you and your missus came running down the path. Thank heaven for shrubbery or you would've spotted me. Imagine my surprise to see you of all people."

"I bet. Then what happened?"

"That boy came flying by after you. The one you hauled in with me."

Charlie tugged his ear. "That's it. You didn't see or hear anyone else?"

Spanky settled back in his chair. "Now I didn't say I didn't hear anyone else. When I finally made it to the tree line, I heard lots of things going on in the forest. Screaming, running, shadows flying all around. The nighttime plays funny tricks on your imagination, you know."

"But the only people you know for sure who were out there were Mitch, Candi, the blonde, me and my wife, and the waiter, Andrew? No one else?

Spanky nodded slowly, "Sounds about right. But like I said before the night can play tricks on your mind. I could've sworn I saw a nymph or two running around in the shadows of the trees.

Chapter 13

The drive home was pleasant with the sun filtering through the tall pines and hardwoods that lined the curvy road leading to the McClung's semi-rural subdivision. The drive home usually gave Charlie time to calm his brain from the day's chaos. But this time, he knew the reason for the turmoil at work waited for him at home. Joan.

All he wanted to do was to grab a bite to eat, and then fall into bed with Marian. But instead, he would have to talk with Joan without mentioning the elephant that would be stomping around the room, pretending it was just another routine day. And he dreaded even more having to take Joan down to the station to question her about Mitch's murder.

"Son, ya need to be gettin' that wrinkle off your brow before ya get home to our Marian."

Charlie smiled weakly. Da's Irish accent always soothed his mind. He was glad Ma and Da never assimilated the American accent. "Yeah, last thing I want to do is to worry Marian any more than she already is." He sighed heavily. "Da, nothing we heard today seemed to clear Joan. What do you think?"

"Well, now, I think Spanky's comment about Candi put a new twist on things."

Charlie scratched the stubble on his chin. "It definitely gives her a motive for wanting Mitch out of her way, but then again why go to such drastic measures, uh?"

"Ay, son, but ya know as well as I do, that some people kill for a lot less of a reason."

"Yep. We're just a couple of miles from home. Let's talk about something more pleasant so I can get rid of this." Charlie pointed to his lined forehead.

"Son, I'm afraid they may be permanent. Ya not a spring chicken anymore."

Charlie laughed. "What are you saying? I'm old? What does that make you?"

"A wise and spry mature man." Da winked. "Ya only as old as ya feel, and your Ma and I we—,"

"No, no, no! I've heard all I need to know." Charlie waved his hand to hush Da. "Don't need any weird images of you and Ma cavorting in my head."

Da shook his head. "Tsk-tsk, son, what a depraved mind ya have." He chuckled. "All I was gonna say was ya Ma and I walk five miles every day."

"Yeah, right." Charlie snorted. "You better be telling the truth, because I'm asking Ma when we get home."

"Well, now, it might not be every day, but ya Ma and I burn some calories."

"Ah, gross, Da. I knew you weren't talking about walking." Charlie laughed. "Thanks, Da, for that image. And I'm still going to ask Ma."

"Well, ya wanted something more pleasant to talk about. And that always brings a smile to my face." Da hooked his thumbs under armpits and grinned. "Go ahead ask ya Ma, son, I've nothing to be embarrassed about."

Charlie glanced at Da still grinning, and thought how fortunate he was to have parents who truly loved each other. "That's okay. I believe you."

He turned into their driveway and parked the police cruiser outside of the three-car garage. When Marian had the house remodeled, she also bought the old Panell house and had it taken down. It was a bitter battle between Marian and the homeowners' association president to have the house demolished. But in the end, with the backing of the homeowners who didn't want a murder house on their street, and the threat of a law suit, the association president grudgingly admitted defeat. Marian used the land to expand the garage, not only to provide Charlie a spacious workshop, but also a place to house his beloved Wilma, a black 1967 Plymouth Belvedere GTX with a 426 hemi.

Da and Charlie entered the kitchen through the garage. When Charlie opened the door, the aroma of coffee, bacon, and French toast welcomed them into the kitchen. He heard Ma's patient voice giving instructions.

"Stir gently now. Ya don't want ya batter to be too stiff or ya crumpets will be blind."

Charlie heard the perfect harmony of Joan's loud and Marian's soft laughter.

"Now we can't have our crumpets without eyes." Charlie stood behind his wife.

"Charlie!" Marian threw her flour-sprinkled arms around her husband.

He picked up his wife and kissed her forehead, and then eased her feet back to the floor. Charlie saw Joan practically cowering in the corner of the spacious kitchen. The despair on her face made his heart sink. The laughter that had filled the kitchen was replaced with silence.

"Joan," was all Charlie said as he held out his hands. She quickly grabbed them as if his hands were her only lifeline to escape a bottomless sea.

Charlie pulled her against his wide chest. Joan's tears spotted his white dress shirt.

"I'm sorry, Charlie." She pulled away and hugged herself. "I'm nothing but trouble."

"Shush, Joan, don't worry about it. I've had the shirt on for way too long." He motioned for her to come back. "Look, you are here with us, your family. Let us take care of you. You've taken care of us."

Marian slid her arm around Joan's waist. "Yeah, how many times have I been trouble for you?" Marian leaned her head against Joan's. "You're my sister by choice. The best kind."

Greasing crumpets rings, Ma said, "Ah, child, we've crumpets to make now."

"Ya gonna be feeding us crumpets for breakfast?" Da complained.

Ma pulled her husband to her side, and then planted a big kiss on his mouth. "And a good morning to ya, too. Now sit down with ya son. We've been keeping Honey Orange French toast warm for ya two. There's plenty of bacon and sausages." She gave Joan a crumpet ring. "Here, now put this on the hot frying pan, and then pour some batter in it. Let's see if it has eyes. Marian, come help her while I tend to these two poor starving lads."

Charlie and Da sat at the small kitchen table that filled the area in front of the large bay window, another feature Marian had expanded during the remodel. As he ate, he watched Marian and Ma draw Joan's focus to the crumpets. Joan's eyes seemed to sparkle whenever a crumpet she flipped had eyes. Ma would plant a kiss on her flipping hand, and Joan would smile, a genuine smile. Each perfectly grilled crumpet that Joan placed on the serving plate was slathered with Irish butter by Marian. The three of them worked like a well-seasoned team.

Charlie moved his clean plate to the side, picked up a mug of coffee, and then leaned back to watch the women. He wondered how long this charade of normalcy would last. And then it happened as the last crumpet was cooked.

"Look at these lovely crumpets, my flower. I must say." Ma rested her fists on her hips as she surveyed the plate of warm crumpets. "I think they're better than mine." Ma gave Joan a tight squeeze to congratulate her on her success.

Joan beamed. "Do you really think so Ma? Are they good enough to serve at The …" Her smile faltered. Joan stood frozen as if she had been caught committing a crime.

She slowly turned away from Ma's embrace. Joan stared at Charlie. "I guess you'll be wanting to talk with me."

Charlie nodded. "Yes, but it can wait." He smiled. "I would love to sample the crumpets that's put Ma's to shame. That's a feat no one, and I mean no one, can claim."

He studied Joan's face, not the face of a cold-blooded murderer. Her tight lips trembled with a hint of a smile. This was the first time he'd seen her sans makeup. She was a natural beauty, like his Marian. Joan's eyes were glassy and reddened from too many tears, he supposed. Her blonde hair was sticking out in places, like someone who just rolled out of bed. She was wearing a thick terrycloth robe, like Marian's except Joan's was a pale pink. It was unlike Joan to be so disheveled.

Charlie stood and pulled out a chair. "Come sit down and bring the crumpets with you." He looked at Marian. "I'd love some jam."

Marian scrambled to the refrigerator and pulled out several jars of jams and jellies.

Joan set the tray of crumpets on the table.

Charlie held out the chair for her. As she sat down, he slid the chair under Joan, and then kissed the top of her head. He winked at Marian as she arranged the jars on the table.

His wife smiled and mouthed the words, "Thank you."

"Ah, Mary Kathleen, I thought I'd never see this day. Ya crumpets bested." Da teased his wife.

Ma playfully slapped her husband's shoulder as she refilled his empty mug with coffee. "Ya better be watching ya tongue or ya be sleeping in the other guestroom."

Coffee sloshed in the carafe as Da pulled Ma close to his side. "Ya know I love ya, me dearie."

"Da and Ma, we'll be having none of that at the table. I'd like to enjoy these fine looking crumpets without all of your lovey-dovey." Charlie punched his father's shoulder.

Marian finished putting plates and napkins on the table and sat down next to Joan.

Everyone enjoyed the crumpets and complimented Joan.

Joan picked at the plain buttered crumpet on her plate. Her hands fell to her lap. Her body trembled as she took a deep breath, and then pressed a napkin to the corners of her eyes.

"Thank you for treating me like nothing has happened." Joan smiled sadly, "But we all know that's not true." She reached over and clutched Charlie's hand. "I need to talk. Now. I need to get this over with." Tears erupted. She pushed away from the table. "I'm sorry. I'm so sorry," she cried as she fled to her bedroom.

Marian ran after her.

"Son, do ya have to take her to the station?" Ma had tears in her eyes.

Charlie nodded.

"Now, love, even though she's like one of our own, ya know things have to be done properly." Da slid his arm around his wife's shoulders, and then kissed her gently on the cheek.

Ma smirked. "I know. I know. I just wish …" She stood. "Let me see if our girls need me."

Charlie rubbed his face with both hands. "Da, have you ever done anything this hard?"

"No, son. That I have not. I don't envy ya one bit."

Chapter 14

Charlie stood with Marian and Ma on the other side of the two-way mirror as they looked at Joan's fragile figure waiting to be interviewed.

"Are you sure I can't sit next to her? I'll be quiet. I promise. I'll hold her hand that's all." Marian pleaded softly.

"You're not her attorney nor is she a child needing an adult." Charlie tapped the tip of his wife's nose with his index finger. "She'll be okay." He turned to leave the room, and then stopped. Charlie looked at Ma. "Take care of each other." He pointed his finger at Marian. "The door to the interview room will be guarded by Da, so don't think about coming in to rescue Joan. Understand?"

"Yes, sir." Marian didn't press her husband. She knew when Charlie's mind was set. Leaning against Ma, they entwined arms for support and comfort.

Charlie approached Officer Thayer and Da waiting for him outside of interview room one.

"Da, do you mind standing guard? Not that I think Marian will try to burst in, but that woman is full of surprises. I love her despite her miniscule faults, really I do."

"I know what ya mean, son. I'll be guarding against ya Ma, too. She can get like a mama bear guarding her cubs."

Memories of Ma charging after a little league coach flooded his brain. He laughed. "Yep, I remember." Charlie reached for the door knob. "Let's get this over with."

Joan flinched at the sound of the opening door. The sight of Charlie and Officer Thayer made her shiver even though the room was warm.

Officer Thayer set a plastic cup filled with ice water on the table. "For you, Miss Delaney."

"Thank you." Joan whispered without making an effort to retrieve the cup.

Charlie sat across from Joan. She looked a bit different from this morning. Since Joan lived in their subdivision, Marian had taken her home to change. Joan had applied makeup, fixed her hair, and was wearing a cream-colored shell with a red blazer and midnight blue jeans. After the makeover, Marian drove her best friend and Ma to the station.

He noticed Joan was devoid of all jewelry and wondered if she did that on purpose because she assumed she'd be jailed. Curious.

"Joan, I'll try my best to make this as quick and painless as I can, but there are few questions I have to ask that may make you uncomfortable. Understand?"

She nodded.

"Miss Delaney, you will need to speak your answers. We are being recorded." Officer Thayer gently instructed her.

Joan's cheeks flushed. "I understand, Chief McClung."

Charlie felt like a jerk. He didn't want Joan to be afraid of him or treat him any differently. But the circumstance of their positions were dramatically altered.

"Okay. Mitch Quinn, the victim, told me you were once married to him. Is that correct?"

Her eyes focused just behind McClung's head at the reflective mirror. "Is she back there? Will she hear all my horrible secrets?" A tear balanced in the corner of her eye.

"Yes, Marian is listening and so is Ma. Would you like for me to ask them to wait in my office?"

Joan shook her head. "No. I'd rather have to only disclose my sins just once. She needs to know. Everyone needs to know." She plopped her elbows on the table, and then buried her face in her hands.

Charlie put the box of tissues next to Joan's elbow and waited for her to compose herself.

After a few seconds, Joan sat up and blotted her face and nose. She looked at the black smear on the tissue and chuckled. "Great, I probably look like a cheap prostitute after a busy night." She turned bright red.

"No, you look just fine, really."

Joan smiled weakly. "Thanks." She bit her lower lip. "Marian's one lucky gal to have you. Unlike me." Joan moaned, "I'm just going to tell it all. Everything. I want y'all to know my sordid past, but …" She hugged herself, sighed heavily, and then looked away. "I've been married three times. My first choice was dubious to say the least." She

116

shrugged, "But the other two were not bad. I just didn't love either of them."

Charlie could just imagine the look on Marian's face. He was shocked, but over the years he had developed a pretty good poker face. It didn't work on Marian though, she could read him no matter how hard he tried.

"So, how did you come to marry Mitch?"

"I was eighteen and stupid. Dazzled by the charm of the king of all snakes." Joan wiped the end of her nose. "Yeah, I thought he was the most handsome and sophisticated man on Earth. He promised I'd be his shining star." She chuckled sadly, "Little did I know at the time what he meant by that.

"How did you two meet?"

Joan tugged at the hair on the nape of her neck. "Well, sir, that was my first mistake. I decided to skip school with one of my girlfriends. We took a cab to downtown Atlanta and walked around. Did stupid stuff. I don't remember exactly where we were when I ran into Mitch. I've tried to forget that part of my life."

She got a faraway look in her eyes. "It's like a bad dream, like it never really happened. But the past has a way of rearing its ugly head just when you thought the evil snake was dead. I guess the old saying is true you've got to cut off the head …"

Joan's attention snapped back to the present. "Anyway," She picked up the cup, sipped, set it down, but continued to hold it. "He told me I was the most beautiful girl he'd ever seen." Joan tapped a bright pink fingernail against the side of the cup. "It was love at first sight for me. We got married after one week."

"What did your parents think?" Charlie made a few notes and waited for Joan's answer.

She swallowed. "Well, I never told them. I just slipped out one night and never went back." Her finger went still. "I did call them to tell them I was okay and I had a job."

Scratching her chin, she paused to keep from crying. "But I don't think they ever gave me a second thought because they never tried to contact me or anything. And yes, I did give them a number where I could be reached." Joan picked up the cup, and then quickly set it down without drinking.

Charlie understood why she bolted into Mitch's arms. She thought she had found love. Love her parents obviously had never shown her. "Joan, would you like a diet Coke or something besides water?"

She giggled nervously. "What I'd really like is a glass of wine, but it's kinda early for that. Yeah, I'll take a diet Coke. That is, if it's not too much trouble."

Charlie looked at Officer Thayer.

The young man hopped up, and then poked his head out of the door and asked Da to get the soda.

"Tell me what happened after you married Mitch."

Joan stared at a water stain on the wooden table. "Things were okay at first. We had a small but nice downtown apartment. I worked as a cocktail waitress in the gentlemen's club where Mitch bartended. After about a month, that's when I realized the marriage was a trap. He said if I didn't dance, he'd kick me out on the streets. That's what he meant when he said he'd make me his star."

"So you became a stripper?"

She nodded slowly. "Yep." Joan looked into Charlie's eyes. "I decided if I had to, I'd be the best one ever. I saw how much money those girls made. I figured if I could save enough, I could bolt one day. I wouldn't need Mitch for nothing."

"And?" Charlie wanted to move the story along.

Joan grinned and wiggled her finger at him. "I see what Marian was talking about. That's okay, I really don't like dwelling on the past, so I'll make this long story short."

Charlie's cheeks turned a light pink. "So it's really that obvious?"

"Uh-huh. So, I became Barbie, the star attraction. I was the club's money maker. Even had to move to a bigger building to hold all our clients." Joan made air quotes when she said the word clients. "Then one night, I took a break outside and this clean-cut man approaches me. He tells me God loves me even though I'm a sinner."

There was a knock on the door. Da entered the room with a can of diet Coke and a large cup of ice. "Here ya go, flower." And then he retreated quickly.

While opening the can, Joan continued, "I don't know why, but for some reason the man's words stuck with me. The next night I went out and there he was. And so to the point, I left one night with him and never went back. I filed for divorce and married that clean-cut man."

"Just like that, you leave Mitch without any troubles from him or the club?"

Joan slowly poured the soda into the cup of ice. "Yeah, I didn't take any money or anything of any value with me. I left empty-handed, just the shirt on my back. Thomas, that was the clean-cut man's name, said he'd provide for my every need. Thomas James Smith made good on his word. I wanted to become a chef. So he paid for my schooling, and helped me get a job in one of the finest restaurants downtown. It didn't hurt that I graduated top of the class with tons of awards and honors."

Charlie smiled. "I guess when you decide to do something you push your way to the top."

"Yeah, but that's not something I'm proud of when it comes to my first job." Joan glanced at Charlie, and then adverted her eyes to the water stain. "Please don't ask me to go into details." She glanced up quickly toward the reflective mirror, and concentrated on the round stain on the table. "Please leave me a little bit of my dignity."

"For now, I don't think those details are pertinent to this case." Charlie scribbled on his notepad. "You said you were married three times. What happened with Thomas?"

Joan pursed her lips. "That's not something I'm proud of either. I loved Thomas, but more like a good friend. We didn't have what you and Marian have or what Ma and Da have. You know, that special connection." She stared at the reflective mirror. "Maybe one day I'll find it. Anyway, I left Thomas after five and a half years to marry a much older, very wealthy man I'd met at the restaurant where I worked at the time." She hesitated. "You know, even though we were only married six months before he died, I think that was the closest I'd ever come to feeling that kind of love." Bobbing her head, she said,

"Yeah, I think so." Joan smirked and shook her head. "Or maybe it was just a father thing."

"Trust me, you will know when you do find it." Charlie was thankful he'd trusted his granny's words and waited for Marian. "I need to ask you some questions about last night. Why did Mitch come to see you?"

Joan looked directly at Charlie. "Money. He needed money. Said if I didn't give it to him, he'd tell you and Marian all of my dirty little secrets."

"Blackmail. How much?"

"He wanted fifty thousand dollars by Monday."

Charlie jotted down the amount. "Did he say why?"

"I asked Mitch if it was his bookie. All he did was grin. Didn't really say the reason."

"Hmm." Charlie could see anger in Joan's eyes and the hate in her voice as she spat out her words. "Do you know Myles Shumaker? He goes by the name of Spanky."

"Yes, but I never got involved in any of Mitch's business dealings. He was just a friend to me. Nothing else. I swear to that. Nothing but a friend. Why? Is he involved in this?"

Charlie wrote down, *Spanky, Mitch - Long-term relationship*. "Let's just say he's in town and he was at The Primrose last night."

"That's who Mitch owed money to." Joan shook her head. "But I can't believe he would stoop to murder."

"What about Candace Evans, goes by Candi?"

"No."

"Do you know of anyone who would want to see him dead?"

Joan threw up her hands. "How should I know that? I haven't seen or heard from Mitch in ... what ... almost twenty years." She collapsed back into her chair.

"Did you cut his throat?"

Horror replaced the anger in her face. "No! I didn't kill him. I didn't!" She started to cry. "He was dead when I got there. I swear it! He was already dead." Joan ran a tissue under her nose. "Tell me, Charlie! Tell me you believe me."

Charlie felt smaller than a grain of sand underneath a pregnant ant. A lump formed in his throat. He could feel Marian's turmoil. "What about in the kitchen? Did you put your knife to his throat?"

Joan wiped her wet cheeks. "You don't believe me?"

"I didn't say that." Charlie sat stone faced. He had no other choice.

Officer Thayer replied softly. "Miss Delaney, this is very difficult for the chief, well for all of us here at the station. Can you please answer the question?"

Joan nodded. "Yes, I did, but I didn't hurt him. It's just ... he made me so angry, taunting me, laughing at me." Her mouth hung open. Her face was red as tears squiggled through her makeup. "Mitch embarrassed me. He called me Barbie in front of Andrew." Joan buried her face in a bed of tissues.

Charlie and Officer Thayer sat in silence and Joan sobbed.

She hiccupped. "I wanted him out of my life permanently. And I knew ... I knew if I gave him the money, he'd keep coming back for more."

"Let's back up a little bit. Tell me how the two of you ended up at that bench."

"We agreed to meet at midnight. I'd give him my answer. It was my idea to meet at the bench because I didn't want anybody to see me with him."

Charlie tugged his earlobe. "But Heather heard everything you and Mitch talked about. Surely, you knew that. And Andrew saw you in the kitchen together."

"No, but ... she said ..." Joan stared just beyond Officer Thayer's head. "She lied. I guess I just wanted to believe her when she said she'd heard nothing." She looked at her hands resting in her lap. "And Andrew ... I knew I could trust him." A tiny smile played with her lips. "He has a little crush on me, but he's a good boy. Harmless."

"Why was your knife at the scene of the crime?" Charlie brought Joan back to reality.

"I don't know. I was stunned to see it on the bench. I thought Mitch brought it with him as a joke or maybe to use it to threaten me. I didn't know he was dead. I thought he was pretending to be asleep because I was late. So I grabbed the knife before he could." Joan's breath became quick and shallow. "I felt something wet on the knife. That's when I saw all the blood. I heard screaming. It was me. I couldn't stop screaming! Oh, God! Oh, God!" Joan grabbed the edge of the chair and gasped for breath.

Outside of the door, Charlie heard Marian's panicked voice and Da and Ma trying to calm her down. He nodded at Officer Thayer. "Let her in."

Officer Thayer opened the door. Marian ran to Joan and knelt beside her best friend. "Joan, come on girl. Take a deep breath through your nose. Exhale through your mouth. Come on. Deep breath, through the nose. Exhale, out the mouth."

Joan obeyed.

"That's a good girl. I'm here. You're safe. Okay? Do you understand? I'm here." Marian looked at her husband's strained face and mouthed the words, *It's okay. I understand.*

Charlie felt the fist squeezing his heart relax its grip.

Joan nodded and leaned against Marian. "I'm sorry. I'm so sorry." She whispered.

"There's nothing to be sorry about. Nothing." Marian stood as Joan clung to her with her arms wrapped around her hips.

"Don't you understand?" Joan cried, "I wanted him dead, Marian. I wanted him dead."

Chapter 15

"What are you doing here? I've got to go on in fifteen." Candi lined her eyes with deep black liner.

Spanky leered at the barely dressed woman young enough to be his daughter. Thoughts drifted in his mind, thoughts he hoped no man had ever had about his daughters. He steered his ideas back to business, the reason why he was in the stripper's private dressing room.

"We have a business proposition which needs to be discussed." Spanky stood behind her chair and stared at their reflection in the vanity mirror.

Candi layered cherry bomb red lipstick on her full lips. She examined her face in the brightly lit mirror, then swirled blush on her bright pink cheeks. "No, I don't think so." She stood blocking Spanky's view.

"Look, I didn't come down here for nothing."

Candi turned. Her large, round, fake breasts were covered with a petite triangle-shaped piece of red sequined fabric. Her skin shimmered and radiated the scent of vanilla and sandalwood.

Spanky licked his dry lips. He pulled a monogrammed handkerchief from his suit pocket, and blotted his sweaty forehead.

"You like these?" Candi supported a breast in each hand and jiggled them. "Mitch bought these as an investment."

He shoved his hands in his coat pockets. "A mighty fine investment, I must say. Which is why I'm here as you know."

Candi threw her long leg up on the chair and folded forward, exposing her bare bottom. "I gotta do my stretches before I go on. Do you mind?"

"Not in the least, but we had a deal which we need to discuss tonight. Right now." Spanky was mad at himself for letting the bimbo get the best of him.

"I don't need your deal anymore. Mitch left me everything." She stood up and leaned toward the right and then the left to stretch the muscles in her sides. A diamond sparkled from her belly button.

"Oh, is that a fact?"

"Yeah, that's a fact." She grinned as she straightened a red lacy garter. "I spoke with his lawyer, a man easily persuaded to divulge privileged client information." She slowly licked her index finger. "If you know what I mean."

Spanky laughed. "You can wipe that smug look off of your painted face. Mitch left you everything you say? Did he know that?"

Candi smirked at the sweaty fat man. "Does it matter now?"

"No, not really. But Mitch had debts. Debts you now own."

"No. I don't think so."

He gently clutched her forearm. "I don't want to bruise the boss's new merchandise."

Candi felt her confidence shake a bit. Maybe she really didn't know what kind of trouble Mitch had gotten himself tangled up in. "What do you mean, new merchandise? I don't belong to nobody any more. Now that Mitch is dead."

"His debts didn't die with him, sweet cheeks. That ain't the way this game is played." He released his grip.

"What? You mean the fifty-thousand dollars?" Her thoughts quickly flew to Mitch's ex-wife, but dismissed it just as fast. Candi didn't want to be anywhere near the murder investigation. She figured she was in the clear. No reason to go stirring up muddy waters.

Spanky's head wobbled side-to-side on his neckless body. "That plus more."

"More!" Candi yelled. "How much more?"

Spanky sauntered around the well-appointed dressing room. "Looks like Mitch was doing better than he let on to the boss." He glanced at Candi. "I guess it's a good thing I paid ol' Mitch a visit. But I think with new management …" He stopped mid stroll and pointed to Candi. "We can do even better."

She narrowed her eyes, her long fake eye lashes nearly coming together. "What do you mean exactly? I own this club now. It said so in the will. I don't need you or any boss. I am the boss!"

"Tsk-tsk. Sadly, no, you're not." He picked up a long strand of pearls that hung to the floor. "I bet you can make these dance." Then he manipulated the unusually long strand of pearls like puppet strings. "Dance little monkey, dance."

Candi marched over in her red-sequined platform stilettos and stood in front of Spanky. "I know what you're insinuating. I look stupid. I act stupid, but I am not stupid!" She snatched the pearls from his hands and flung them across the room.

Spanky held his sausage-like finger to his lips. "Shhh, no need to get angry. No need for raised voices. I never said you were stupid." He shrugged. "Maybe misinformed or ill-advised by Mitch's attorney, perhaps."

Candi gaped at Spanky as her eyes fluttered. Her mind whirled trying to figure out what she'd gotten herself mixed up in. Maybe she wasn't as clever as she thought she was, apparently there was one element she had overlooked.

"Please," he pulled out the dressing table chair, "sit and I can tell you briefly Mitch's business arrangements with us." He looked at his Rolex. "We have roughly seven minutes before you go on."

Candi eased down slowly onto the padded velvet chair.

"That's right. First of all, let me congratulate you on our new partnership." He patted the top of her poufy platinum-blonde head. "You showed Mitch who wore the pants in this relationship." Spanky smirked. "Now, I won't ask you any questions about how you arranged things."

Confused, she looked at Spanky. "What?"

Spanky arched an eyebrow and ran a finger across his sweaty neck.

"No, I didn't kill Mitch."

"Of course not, dear. Of course not." He lightly tapped her cheek with his fingertips. "No reason to soil your hands, right?"

Candi stared without comment at Spanky.

"I'll put this in succinct and simple terms. Mitch was, on paper, the owner. But what the attorney failed to reveal to you is there is a loan agreement held by my boss who lives in Virginia. A loan that has not been paid back in full." He snapped his fingers in front of Candi's unblinking eyes. "Are you with me? Do you understand?"

"Yeah, I do. I'm up a never-ending creek without a paddle."

"I wouldn't say that. My boss is a fair man. I'm sure a new loan agreement can be brokered."

Candi snorted. "I bet. You'll bleed me dry."

"No, no, no. Like I said, my boss is a fair and generous man. You work hard. Your girls work hard. Grow your business. You're just a baby. You'll have it paid off before you see your first gray hair." His fingertips brushed a stray lock of hair from her forehead. An oversized silver and diamond earring swung from her earlobe as he tucked the strands behind her ear.

"Generous, huh?" Candi grinned. "I can be too, you know. Maybe we can help each other. You know, you scratch my back and I'll scratch yours."

Spanky chuckled. "Yeah, you get the picture. I like the way you think. Well, I'll be out there watching the show."

She stood and snapped her garter. "I better see some twenties. Better not be any dollar bills."

Spanky looked her over. "With a body like that, I bet you'll see ol' Andrew Jackson staring at you a lot."

Someone knocked on her door and yelled, "Three minutes, Miss Candi, three minutes."

"I'll be seeing you after the show."

Candi looked at her reflection one more time before she stepped out. "Okay, but give me thirty minutes to get freshened up before you come back."

"Whatever you say. I'll be bringing a bottle of champagne to celebrate our new relationship."

She swirled a chubby brush around her face. "Sure, fine, sounds great."

Spanky walked out of the brightly lit dressing room into a shadowed hallway. He thought he heard someone walk behind him. He turned. "Who's there?" He could have sworn he saw someone duck into a side room. Shaking his head, he mumbled to himself and tapped his temple, "The darkness plays tricks on the old gray cells."

Candi strutted into her dressing room and closed the door. She sat on a zebra print chaise and unbuckled her stilettos, then carefully placed them in the shoe closet Mitch had custom built for her. "Gonna miss ol' Mitch, but a girl's gotta do what she needs to do to survive in a man's world." She spoke softly as she ran her hand down the shoe closet door. "I bet Miss High and Mighty never had one of these. Probably because she had only one pair of shoes." Candi laughed out loud.

She picked up the pearls she had tossed across the room. They were fake, but who in the audience cared? They only wanted to see how she used them. Candi liked the way they felt on her soft white skin. She ran them up her firm inner thigh and across her toned belly.

Candi sat on the velvet chair in front of the makeup vanity. She placed the pearls in an alabaster bowl from Egypt, a gift from one of her gentlemen friends. He said when he saw it during a business trip, he thought of her delicious milky skin.

Glancing around the room, she spied many gifts from many different men. Candi smiled. She felt like the luckiest woman on Earth. So many generous admirers who made her feel like a queen deserving of their adoration and expensive offerings.

She admired the gift sitting on the vanity from one of her fans, an ornate golden clock with an angel lounging on its top. It reminded her Spanky would be arriving soon with chilled champagne in hand. It wouldn't take her long to get ready. All she was wearing were two red garters stuffed with bills. The rest of her apparel had been abandoned on stage. Someone would bring it to her once they had cleaned it. Dancing was a sweaty profession.

She pulled the money from the garters, pleased to see so many large bills, like Spanky had supposed. The odd dollar bill or two made her eyes roll with disgust. Candi straightened the bills all facing the same way, then sorted them by denomination. Next, she opened a small wall safe behind an exquisite print of *Ceres At A Fountain, Attended by Putti,* and carefully put the money inside.

Candi went behind a room divider with a cherry blossom print. She wiped her body free from perspiration with pre-moistened cloths, tossing them into a wicker basket to be emptied later. Continuing with her at-the-club cleansing ritual, Candi smoothed lotion on her skin, followed with a delicate dusting of powder.

Someone knocked on the door as she was slipping on a long, white, very low-cut, sheer negligee. "Go away! I said thirty minutes, Spanky. You'll have to wait!"

There was no reply, but another knock.

Candi took a deep breath and counted to five. She couldn't afford to offend Spanky, not now anyway. It was way too early in their new business partnership. She'd have to test the waters to know how far she could go without a riptide yanking her to the point of no return.

"Just a minute! I'm almost ready." She flung on the matching robe leaving it open and slipped her feet into a pair of white spiked-heeled feathery evening mules. She raced to the vanity, roped on the pearls and removed the silver and diamond dangles from her earlobes, and replaced them with a long cluster of pearls.

"Be there in a sec." Candi swiped her lips with red lipstick, and then sauntered to the door.

She smiled seductively and opened the door. Her smile quickly melted. "What are you doing here? I told you to never come here again. Remember?"

"You didn't call me like you said you would."

Candi tried to shut the door. The intruder's foot held the door open as they easily pushed their way in, causing Candi to stumble backward. She landed on the white furry rug lying in front of the zebra print chaise.

Normally, Candi didn't mind being on the rug, but this wasn't that kind of rendezvous. She scrambled to her feet and kicked her shoes at the unwelcomed guest. The first shoe took them by surprise, hitting their chest. The second one was caught mid-air.

The intruder walked toward Candi. "We had a deal."

Candi was angry. No one treated her like this, especially some two-bit punk. She lunged at the visitor who quickly side-stepped her and smacked Candi's butt with the shoe.

"Crap that hurt!" Candi whined as she rubbed her stinging bottom. "That better not make a bruise or—"

"Or what, Candace, or what?"

Candi sat down on the padded vanity chair. "Don't call me that."

"Candace, Candace, Candace," chanted the uninvited caller. "Why not? It's your birth name."

Candi glared at the intruder. "I don't care what you call me. Just get out of here. I have a gentleman that will be here any minute now. We can talk later. Just leave. Now!"

"You mean Spanky?"

Candi's nostrils flared and her eyes widened.

"Yeah, I know all about Spanky. What? You're embarrassed for him to find out you are close to someone like me? Huh, Candace?"

Candi grinned nervously. "No, not at all. It's just … uh … there's been a twist in our scheme. Yeah, and not a good one." Candi reached for one of the bottom drawers to the dressing table.

"Nope, don't do that. I'll get whatever it is in the drawer." The trespasser opened the deep drawer. "Ah, libations. Thank you for your hospitality, Candace. Let's see what we have here." The intruder pulled out three bottles, whiskey, vodka, and brandy. "Whiskey, shall we? A toast to us."

"Okay, but only one finger for me. Spanky's bringing champagne."

The intruder poured the drinks, handed one to Candi, and then sipped the other one. "I'll go, for now that is, if you give me what was so lovingly put into your pretty little garters."

Candi choked. "All of it?"

"Yes, all of it. Besides, you'll get even more tonight during your second performance. The little perverts will be slap-happy drunk and freer with their money."

Candi sipped in silence.

"I watched your show. You're quite talented." The uninvited guest finished the whiskey. "Now, give me the money and I'll be on my way before Spanky gets here. We can discuss our arrangement tomorrow." The interloper stood behind Candi and looked in the mirror. "Although, I am a little upset you won't introduce me to your friend. Makes me sad. But then again, I've always been a sore subject to you and your mother."

"Fine!" Candi stood and carried her drink to the hidden wall safe. The intruder followed.

Candi swung away the picture to reveal the safe. She set the tumbler on a small side table under the print. Opening the safe, she asked, "Why after all these years do you want to be part of my life? Do you think you're going to leach off of me for the rest of your life?"

"Shut-up and give me the money. We can discuss the ins and outs of our future together as a family."

Candi picked up the tumbler and flung the whiskey at her tormenter, and then tried to run.

The intruder grabbed Candi by her long hair as she tried to run past. "Ah, now that's not nice." The intruder twisted Candi's hair and shoved her back to the padded chair, forcing her to sit.

"You think you can man-handle me to get what you want? I've swam in waters with bigger sharks than you and survived. So think again. You won't get a dime from me. Do you understand? Never!" Candi reached for a pair of scissors hidden under a scarf lying on the vanity.

Her tormentor used her hair to jerk her back against the chair, and then wrapped Candi's hair around her neck.

Candi felt her beautiful hair tighten, cutting off her air supply.

"Are you going to play nice and give me that money? Are you going to tell the world about us? Are you going treat me like …" The tormenter paused, leaned down, cheek to cheek with Candi and stared at their reflections in the mirror, Candi wide eyed, her tormentor with a lopsided smile. The tormentor lightly kissed the top of Candi's ear and whispered, "Are you going to treat me like a close friend, a really close friend?"

Candi shook her head and croaked, "You're not ..." She stretched her arm toward the scarf and with the other hand tried to pull her hair away from her throat.

"What are you looking for under that flimsy little scarf? Do you use that as a prop for one of your shows? Do you want to dance for me?"

Candi continued to strain against the intruder's grip.

"No need to struggle. I'll get it for you."

Candi's face contorted in terror.

Her tormentor leaned forward to retrieve the scarf which was just enough for Candi to grab the scissors.

Candi blindly stabbed at her tormentor who laughed at her lame attempt.

"What? Are you trying to trim your hair?"

She rasped, "No, don't cut my hair. Please." She decided to stop her struggle. Then maybe the intruder would go away. "I'll give you the money," she managed to squeak out.

Her tormentor eased the pull on her hair. "Okay, but first, I'll need these." They reached for the scissors.

Candi again tried to stab her tormentor.

The intruder wrestled the scissors from her hand. "Liar! You're such a liar!" The bully pressed their lips against Candi's ear and whispered, "You're nothing but a lying slut. Always have been."

Candi cried.

The bully gently ran the scissors down her cheek. "Keep crying, I like it."

Candi's tormenter eased the pressure around her throat. "Please don't hurt me. Please. I promise. I'll give you the money. Just let me go."

The bully cocked their head to one side then to the other side. "Well, this will be your third chance. You know what happens if you screw up your third chance."

Candi nodded.

The bully unwrapped the hair from around Candi's neck, but continued to hold it. Using her hair like a rope, Candi was led to the safe. The scissors held tightly in the other hand.

Candi opened it and threw the money on the chaise. "Now leave me. Never come back!"

"Ah, now that's not what I wanted to hear."

Candi watched in horror as her tormentor snipped off a huge lock of her hair, and then flung it up into the air. The fine hair floated down and scattered on the chaise like a platinum cobweb. She shoved the bully away and made for the door.

The intruder laughed. Still holding Candi's hair and yanked her backward.

Candi landed hard on her butt.

"Get up!"

Candi obeyed.

"Sit."

Candi walked back to the makeup dresser and sat.

"Do you want to know how your mother died?"

Candi looked surprised. "What?"

"Yes, unfortunately she told me to get lost, too."

Candi swallowed hard.

"Or better yet, your lover, Mitch?"

"Don't bother. I saw—," Candi felt the bite of the scissors plunge into her neck. Her murderer held the scissors, pushing them deeper. Candi made a feeble attempt to grab them from her neck and watched in the mirror as the blood ran down her neck, ruining her favorite negligee.

Chapter 16

Charlie had a restless night. Marian spent the night at Joan's house, it was the first time without his wife beside him in bed since they married on September twelfth. Even though it was only a little over a month ago, he didn't like it at all. But Joan didn't want to stay with them, which he understood. Of course, Marian couldn't leave Joan alone, the Mitch fiasco was still too fresh.

Marian arrived home just as he and Da were leaving for the station. They had a lingering embrace and passionate kiss before he drove away, leaving behind his one desire.

Charlie sat at his desk as he read over the findings from the crime scene that were just handed to him. There were a few details that were worrisome. First, there was one set of vague and spotty footprints which led toward to the bench where Mitch sat, unknowingly, waiting to be slaughtered. The prints were not well-defined. It was hard to derive any information from them, only that some person was in the woods and walked toward the bench, but where did they come from? The person might as well have parachuted into the forest.

The second detail was another two sets of footprints in the trees across from the bench. Both sets were distinct, one was obviously someone who was barefoot. Candi. It had to be Candi. The footprints didn't go all the way to the edge of the tree line across from where Mitch sat, but the person did have a direct sightline toward the bench. If it was Candi, she could have witnessed Mitch's murder.

Charlie sat back into the leather chair and thought of several reasons why Candi kept silent. He retrieved his notepad and jotted them down.

He continued to read the report. The third set of prints were further back from the barefoot prints, but the person also had a view of the area where Mitch was killed. The next piece of evidence caused the hair on the back of Charlie's neck to stand to attention; pieces of torn paper arranged in an asymmetrical heart.

Charlie flipped through the pictures. There it was, just like the one on the cruise ship. Less than a month ago during their honeymoon cruise, he and Marian sat in a practically empty, dimly lit bar when she noticed someone watching them. When Charlie went to investigate the stranger, the vacant chair was still warm and a misshaped torn paper heart was left on the small round table. He dropped the picture on his desk. Charlie jumped up and walked to stare out of the window. His first instinct was to order twenty-four hour police protection for Marian. Running his hands over the top of his head, Charlie paced in front of his desk.

He stopped. His hands settled on his waistband, fingers drumming on the butt of his gun. Charlie's jaws bulged as he fought the feelings of anger and panic, as rationality struggled for control. Rationality won. He inhaled deeply and sighed. "Maybe it's me they're after," he mumbled, "I pray that's so."

Charlie sat down and finished reading the report. He was waiting for Jack's autopsy report and for Stewie's findings on the four suspects. He closed the folder.

Charlie looked at photographs on his desk. He stared at the one that had been taken of himself and Marian at their wedding reception. He remembered he had pulled Marian to one side for a moment of solitude. They didn't think anyone was aware they were no longer among the crowd. The photographer snapped the picture just before they kissed. She was the love of his life. She was his life. He felt a lump in his throat and a sting in his eyes at the idea that she could be... He couldn't finish the thought. Instead, he picked up the phone.

"Hey!" His heart skipped a beat at the sound of his wife's voice. "Just checking in. Making sure everything is all right."

"What's wrong with me? Nothing, sweetie, I just wanted to hear your voice." Charlie hoped Marian didn't pick up on the lie. "How's Joan?"

"Yeah, well, I'm glad she's feeling hopeful. And a pan of cranberry-nut fudge will make her happy. Make sure you save a few pieces of fudge for me." Charlie had learned early on that Joan had a weakness for dark chocolate and Marian was her enabler. "What are you and Ma going to do today?" Charlie was relieved to hear they were going to hang around the house.

"I don't know when we will be home." He prayed it was before dark. I won't come home for lunch. I'll call you right before Da and I leave for home."

"Okay. I love you, too." Charlie wanted to tell her to keep her gun within reach but he didn't want to worry her. He hung up the phone, happy just to hear her voice.

Officer Thayer poked his head into his office. "Chief, officers Willard and Marshall are back from the crime scene and waiting in the war room. Are you ready?"

"Yes. Are Stewie and Jenny there, too?"

"Yes, sir, and Doctor Jackson should be arriving shortly."

Charlie walked with Thayer to the war room. "Before I go in, please tell me someone besides Stewie made the coffee."

The young officer laughed. "Yes, sir. Made it myself."

As they entered the room, Charlie overheard Stewie complain about the weak coffee.

The officers stood as Charlie entered. Even Da.

"Please, sit down. Thank you, but you don't have to stand every time you see me." He looked at Da, smiled and shook his head.

The officers sat down collectively.

Officer Thayer stood by the whiteboard attached to the wall in front of the long rectangular table. He had each of the four suspects' mug shots posted on the board. Three folders were in front of each officer.

Charlie addressed the men as he paced in front of the whiteboard. "All of you were at the crime scene, so you all know what is in one of the folders. One of the two other folders contains Stewie's findings on our four suspects, and the other folder has the statements and interviews from each of our suspects. Doctor Jackson will be here soon with the autopsy report. Stewie, enlighten us."

Each man opened the folder Stewie had provided.

"Let's start with Andrew Aaron Johnston. He's thirty-one. Arrested for grand theft auto in 1977 and served less than five years of a seven year sentence. When he was released, he went to work as a waiter at The Primrose. He's been employed there for roughly three months. Never married. No children. No family in Georgia. He is originally from Mississippi."

Charlie's finger stabbed the state's name on Andrew's dossier as Stewie read it. "Wait a minute!" He quickly thumbed through the profiles. "Heather, the waitress, said she's from Mississippi."

"That's right, Chief." Stewie cleared his throat. "But it gets more interesting. So is Candace Marie Evans." The thin man held up his long index finger. "But they're not all from the same county."

"Go on, Stewie, don't hold us in suspense. I can see you have more." Charlie was eager to get this case solved.

"Candace Evans is from Newtown, roughly the center of the state, and Heather Neeley is from Sidewinder, east of Newtown. Andrew Johnston is from Jason County, south of Newtown."

"Hmm, not from the same counties but clustered together. Interesting." Charlie tugged his ear. "How old are they?"

Stewie answered from memory. "Andrew is thirty-one. Candace and Heather are both twenty-five. Candace is older than Heather by ten months."

"Anything else on these three?"

"Not much more, but then again, I really haven't had a lot of time to look under all of the rocks. Andrew's been in Georgia since he left high school to attend University of Georgia. Dropped out first quarter. Not sure why, his grades were excellent. Candace came to Atlanta right after high school as well and looks like she went to work at Ken's as soon as she arrived. Heather has lived in Mississippi all of her life. The first record I see of her being in Georgia was almost three weeks ago when she went to work for The Primrose."

"Address. Do we have an address for her, yet?" Charlie was itching to speak with her father.

Stewie shook his head. "No, not yet."

Charlie pointed at Officer Thayer. "That tail we put on her after she left the station. Anything come from that?"

"No, sir. We've tried several times to follow her." Officer Thayer sucked his teeth and tapped the table with his pen. "That girl is a slippery one."

The newest recruit seated at the table raised his hand.

Charlie acknowledged him. "Yes, Officer Marshall?"

"So the only thing any of them have in common is The Primrose and Mississippi. What about Miss Delaney? Is she from Mississippi?"

Stewie answered, "No, born and raised in Georgia. And by the way, she's never been arrested, not even a traffic violation. Candace Evans doesn't have a record, but numerous speeding tickets. Heather has no record. I can't even find a driver's license for her."

"Let's not get into the details of the illustrious Myles Shumaker, also well known as Spanky. He has a long list of offenses, but he's never committed murder."

Da spoke, "Aye, but he's been suspected of ordering hits."

"That's true. He could've arranged it. But if ... no, let's address the obvious points before we start to speculate." Charlie looked at the whiteboard. He wanted to discuss the bits of white paper, but that would have to come in due time. "First, let's write under each one what they have in common."

There was a knock on the door. The station's receptionist, Penny, peered through the long narrow window in the door.

Charlie knew it couldn't be good if she had abandoned her post and he prayed whatever the bad news was it didn't concern Marian.

Penny opened the door, but didn't enter. "Chief, I'm so sorry to disturb you, but I received two calls, back to back, and I thought you would want to know about them ASAP."

"Marian?" Charlie tried to control the fear in his voice.

"No, chief. Doctor Jack Jackson and Atlanta detective Lawrence Hall. It's about one of your suspects, Candi. She's dead."

Charlie wasn't surprised to see patrons trying to get inside Ken's Playhouse at ten o'clock in the morning. The two officers standing guard at its entrance didn't deter them either. The gentleman's club was famous for their healthy and beautiful exotic dancers. He and Officer Thayer flashed their badges and were allowed to pass.

Da had decided to sit out this adventure to go home and be with Ma and Marian. Charlie was relieved, but not because he didn't want his father with him, but because Marian now had Da for protection. After Charlie told his father of his uneasiness, Da was more than happy to be his new daughter-in-law's guardian angel.

The club was mostly empty. Charlie figured most of the clients slithered out before the police had arrived. He recognized one lone figure sitting at the bar with an officer. Spanky.

"Well, Spanky, seems like people just drop dead when you're around."

The large man snarled. "You think you're a funny man, huh? You're just like your old man." Spanky looked around. "Where is that moldy-oldie?"

Charlie ignored him and instead asked the officer where he could find Detective Hall.

The deputy pointed toward a door just beyond the stage.

Charlie left without another word to Spanky. He and Officer Thayer made their way through the curtained door and down a dim, narrow hallway. They stopped outside of the last room on the right. An officer stood guard. Charlie could hear the crime scene crew inside of the brightly lit room taking orders from a man with a deep gravelly voice.

"I'm Chief McClung of Lyman County. Detective Hall called me. He said one of my cards was found at the crime scene."

The aging officer guarding the entrance leaned inside the dressing room. "Boss! Chief McClung here to see you."

When the detective exited the room, Charlie thought he was meeting Dick Tracy. Detective Hall extended his hand. "Chief, I'm happy to see you here so soon."

Charlie returned his firm grip. "Thank you for calling me. Your victim was a suspect in a murder I'm investigating."

"Well, looks like you just narrowed down your list by one." Detective Hall removed his hat and fanned the sweat beading on his face.

Charlie scratched his chin. "Yeah. That fat man, sitting at the bar with one of your men, what's he got to do with this?"

"He found her. You know the guy?" The detective flipped back a couple of pages in the notepad he held.

"Yes. His name's Myles Ely Shumaker. Goes by Spanky. I know him from my days in the Richmond vice squad."

The detective found the page he was looking for. "Yeah, that's the name he gave me. Said he was here on business. He also said he didn't see anything or hear anything."

"How was she killed?"

The Dick Tracy look-alike grimaced as he shook his head. "A pair of scissors right into the jugular. Poor girl watched herself die."

"What do you mean?" Charlie knew it was the same killer. It had to be.

The detective motioned Charlie to enter the dressing room. "We found her sitting at her dressing table. Eyes wide open staring into the mirror."

Charlie noticed fingerprint dust covering nearly every surface. He pointed to the open wall safe. "You think the motive is robbery?"

"Leaning that way. The safe is empty except for a few pieces of jewelry." Detective Hall used his pen to draw Charlie's attention to the remaining jewels. "They're only of moderate value. Nothing to get excited about."

"This room was her private dressing room? No one else used it?" Charlie was impressed with Candi's status.

"Yep, all of the other girls shared rooms."

"She must have been the star she claimed she was to have such nice quarters." Charlie took mental note of the expensive trinkets and furnishings. "Do you think any of the girls would kill for this room?"

"Nah, they said they all got along. Even the bartenders agreed. One big happy family if you can believe it." Detective Hall smirked.

Charlie didn't believe it. This was a dog-eat-dog business. He scanned the room, taking time to memorize details. "You say nobody heard or saw anything?"

"That's the story and they're all sticking to it."

"How do you think the perp got in unnoticed?"

Detective Hall motioned Charlie to follow him. "Anybody could have walked in. I'm surprised this is the first trouble they've had."

About fifteen feet from Candi's room, was a heavy metal door which opened out into a tiny strip of space, not big enough to call an alley. It was a make-shift courtyard with one wonky folding chair sitting in a sea of cigarette butts. The sides of the buildings were covered in profane graffiti. Charlie supposed the area was for the girls to air out.

"Somebody could have entered from either side." The Atlanta detective pointed toward the sunlight sneaking in through narrow spaces in between the tall buildings. "That way leads to a parking lot," he pointed to the left, then he pointed to the right, "That leads to an alleyway. At the end, if you turn right, it goes out to the street in front of Ken's. To the left, leads to the street in front of this," Detective Hall pointed to the building directly behind Ken's Playhouse, "a lingerie and sex shop."

"Very convenient for the girls." Charlie grunted.

Detective Hall went back into Ken's. "And of course the girls leave the door unlocked, easier for them to sneak in if they're late, among other things." He tapped the side of his nose and winked.

"So, you're thinking someone sneaked in to steal the cash from Candi's safe, and then killed her."

"Yep."

"Hmm, it had to be someone who had been in her room before and they had to know about the safe. A client perhaps." Charlie's first thought was Spanky. He was already mad at Candi and he wanted the money Mitch had promised him. "Got any suspects?"

"Just that fat guy out there." Detective Hall shoved his notepad into the pocket of his trench coat. "Look, do me a solid. I'm thinking since you already have these two, the vic and him, as part of your investigation, that we could share information. Maybe the two crimes are related. Maybe not."

The detective took off his hat, and then fanned himself. "I'm retiring at the end of the month. I'd like for my last case to be closed. That guy threatened to sue me if I haul him in. Said I've nothing on him." He shrugged. "He's got a point. I don't have nothing. Not one worthwhile clue. Mmm, maybe if we can get any viable prints from the scissors."

Charlie really wanted to interview Spanky again. "Mind if I question Spanky?"

"Be my guest. Take him with you. Since you two have a history, maybe he'll be more cooperative with you." Hall took out a card from inside his coat. "Here's my number."

Charlie exchanged cards. "Here's another one of mine, since the one you found is now evidence."

Officer Thayer trailed behind the two long-time officers as they walked toward the bar where Spanky sat, drinking a cup of coffee.

"A cuppa for you three fine and upstanding officers of the law? It's decent coffee? What do you say? My treat."

Charlie and Detective Hall sat on either side of Spanky. Officer Thayer sat beside his chief.

"Thank you. I'd like that." Charlie accepted his offer.

Spanky snapped his fingers to get the bartender's attention, held up three fingers, and then pointed down toward his mug.

"You're in a pretty good mood, considering your star has just been murdered."

Spanky sipped his coffee. "Mmm, well, no reason to get upset. Life has a funny way of working things out."

The bartender set down three cups of steaming coffee. "Cream? Sugar?"

Charlie and Officer Thayer waved them away, but Hall accepted. He watched the detective splash seven spoons of sugar into the regular sized cup, and then pour in a generous amount of cream, making the black coffee a pale tan color.

Spanky laughed as he handed the bartender a twenty. "You've got some kind of sweet tooth there."

Detective Hall ignored him and drank his sugar fix.

"Hmm, this is good coffee." Charlie took another sip before he spoke. "Spanky, how would you like to ride back with me and Officer Thayer to our neck of the woods?" He had to find out what Spanky meant by *working things out*.

Spanky finished his coffee. "Ah, I must decline. I will be attending Giuseppe Verdi's Rigoletto at the Fox Theater tonight."

Charlie was impressed. "I've never thought of you as a lover of opera."

"There's many things you don't know about me, McClung, many things."

Charlie nodded. "Probably so, but I'd like to learn more. What if we have you back in time to the opera?" He looked at Officer Thayer. "We can make that promise, right?"

Officer Thayer leaned forward to look at Spanky. "Sure thing. What do you say?"

"Perhaps, let me think about it while I drink another cup of coffee provided by this fine establishment."

Chapter 17

Charlie had to call Marian before they left Ken's Playhouse with Spanky in tow. All was well at the home front. She told him Joan decided to go to The Primrose even though she knew her restaurant was in good hands with Tony and Nick, who had been with The Primrose since the day it opened six years ago. Marian said Joan needed something to keep her mind occupied, but she promised she'd be home before dark. Marian also told him Jack called looking for him, and he'd bring the reports to the station.

He briefly spoke with Da who reported nothing out of the ordinary going on or around the house. Da let him know that Ma was going to make Steak and Guinness pie for supper and she'd already started a Chocolate Orange Guinness cake for dessert.

Charlie's stomach growled. He wanted desperately to be home in time for dinner.

On the way to the station, Spanky slept for most of the ride. It gave Charlie plenty of time to think about his approach for the second interview. Officer Thayer was also quiet as he drove the squad car. Every now and then he'd point out something of interest since Charlie had only lived in Georgia for four months.

When the three men entered the station, Penny Parkinson greeted them. "Hey! Chief, Jack Jackson is waiting for you in your office. He arrived about five minutes ago."

Charlie gave her a thumbs up. "Thanks, Penny, you're the best."

The young girl blushed.

"Thayer, take Spanky to interview one. I'm going to speak to Jack first."

"Yes, sir." Officer Thayer led Spanky down the hallway.

Charlie decided to stop by the office Stewie and Jenny shared. "What's shaking?"

Stewie responded with his usual, "All four cheeks and a couple of chins."

Jenny rolled her eyes.

"You guys have anything new to report?" Charlie compared the desks of his two computer geniuses. Jenny's was best described as chaos and Stewie's was more of an organized chaos.

Stewie whipped around. "Jenny, tell him what you found."

Her round face lit up. "It may not be anything but Heather Morana Neeley appears to have been adopted. I'm working with your brother to get the sealed records opened." Jenny pointed to Stewie. "Your discovery is more exciting."

The corner of Stewie's mouth twitched slightly into what one could possibly call a smile. "Interesting fact. Andrew's father was briefly married to Candi's mother. Four months, that's all."

Charlie slapped his forehead. "What! Why didn't Andrew tell us?"

"That's probably because he doesn't know." Stewie stared at Charlie. "He was only five at the time. And one little nugget I failed to mention is that Andrew's parents remarried a few months later."

Charlie felt a headache developing in his right temple. "All right, get all of this written up and on my desk. I need some time to sort all of this out."

Jenny giggled. "On your desk, Chief."

"Great work guys. Keep digging." Charlie headed up the back stairs. He found Jack in his office, staring out of the window.

"Hey, Jack, my man. How's it going?" The two men shook hands.

"Overworked, but glad for the job security. Man, I tell you, these past two days have been crazy to say the least. Crazy!"

Charlie sat behind his desk and motioned for Jack to sit. "Makes life interesting for sure, but I could stand some boredom." He exhaled heavily. "I've got Spanky in for another interview concerning Candi's death. Did you find anything interesting I should know about?"

Jack shook his head. "Sad to say, no." He hunched up his shoulders. "Well, except whoever killed Mitch and Candi were very skilled. They knew exactly where the kill spots were."

"So you think the same person killed both of them?"

"I'd say yes, simply because of the connection between the two and the fact they were murdered in a seated position."

Charlie moaned. "You're killing me. That's it?"

"Mitch was a time bomb waiting to explode. His heart and liver were shot from years of cocaine and alcohol. I found way too much in his system. Loads of it."

Charlie opened the middle desk drawer and pulled out a bottle of aspirin. "You didn't make my headache any better." He stood. "You have anywhere you need to be right now?"

Jack stood with him. "Nope. What do you have in mind?"

"Come watch the interview with Spanky. After that, dinner at my house." Charlie paused. "Let me make a quick call first."

He dialed his home number. "Hey, sweetie. I've got Jack here. Any reason he can't come for dinner?"

Jack watched Charlie's face light up when he heard Marian's voice. He hoped one day he'd have that kind of woman in his life who would make his face glow.

"No, great. Will Joan be joining us?"

Jack's heart skipped a beat at mention of Joan.

Charlie looked at Jack and shook his head. "Too bad. Maybe after all of this is over, we can all finally get together." He chuckled. "Yeah, matchmakers. Love you. See you soon."

"All right, let's get this over with. Ma's cooking up Steak and Guinness pie and I don't want to miss it."

The two men started out of the office. Jack picked up the bottle of aspirin. "Don't forget these."

"Yeah, I'll need them before I question Spanky."

As soon as Charlie opened the door, he heard Spanky complain he didn't want to be late for the opening curtain.

"And you're not going to be. I want to get out of here as much as you do, if not more." Charlie plopped heavily into the chair and slammed down a folder. "Now, tell me what happened last night after you left here."

Spanky placed his meaty hands on the table, fingers splayed open. "I went back to my hotel, The Georgian Terrace."

Officer Thayer replied, "That's a nice place. Right across the street from the Fox."

"Your boss treats you right." Charlie watched Spanky grin smugly.

Spanky inspected his manicured fingernails. "I've worked hard to get where I am. The boss appreciates my services."

"I'm sure he does." Charlies lightly patted the tabletop. "What next?"

"I decided to pay Candi a visit so we could discuss our business. I arrived an hour or so before her first performance." Spanky leered. "Oh, my, and what a performance it was." He clicked his tongue. "What a valuable asset, lost senselessly."

"Yeah, Spanky, you looked all choked up," Charlie commented sarcastically.

"One has to hide their emotions in my line of work. But to get to the point. She seemed to be under the notion now that Mitch was dead, she owned his club." He shook his head. "Tsk, tsk. But I enlightened

157

her and we had things all straightened out. I had planned to meet her in her dressing room thirty minutes after her show. I even had champagne to toast our new business relationship."

"So you watched her performance. I bet she had a lot of cash in her garters by the end of it. Yeah?"

"More than any stripper I've ever seen. Pity to lose such talent."

Charlie shifted, leaned back comfortably, and propped his left ankle on his right knee. "Hmm, I'm beginning to think maybe Candi wasn't very impressed with your proposed business arrangement. Maybe she didn't want to share her hard earned money." He shrugged. "I'm thinking she disrespected you one too many times. And you …" Charlie pretended to stab himself in the neck.

Spanky's eyes narrowed, his nostrils flared as he clenched his jaws, but sat in silence.

"Am I right? I mean, girls like her are a dime a dozen. You really didn't need her, just like you didn't need Mitch." Charlie crossed his arms and grinned. "Yeah, that's what you meant earlier when you said, life has a way of working out things."

Charlie pointed his finger at Spanky. "You're going to take over the business. Yeah, you are."

Spanky smirked. "Yeah, so what if I am? It doesn't mean I killed them."

"Of course not. Why dirty your soft hands? Yeah?" Charlie looked at Officer Thayer. "What do you think?"

Officer Thayer sighed, "Well, the way I see it, things are pretty cut and dry. In my opinion, Spanky knew he wasn't getting the money from Mitch. And Candi wasn't going to play nice. So he killed both of them because he didn't need them anyway. They were stumbling stones in his way to the top."

Spanky clapped his pudgy hands. "Bravo. You two should write crime novels. I'm sure they'd sell well from the bargain bin." He settled his hands on his thighs, and then stood. "I have an opera to attend as you well know."

"Oh, no, Spanky. We're not finished." Charlie tapped the table. "Sit. Please. You'll be back in your swanky hotel in time to get ready for the opera."

Spanky thudded down in the chair.

"Who did you hire to kill Mitch and Candi?"

"I didn't hire anyone to kill them nor did I kill them." Spanky licked his thick lips. "Are you going to continue to badger me about something I'm not remotely involved in?

Charlie snorted. "Oh, I won't say you're not involved." He held up his fist with his index finger extended. "One. You knew both of them." The next finger pops up. "Two. You were the last person to see them before they died." The third finger raised. "Three. You wanted them out of the way so you could take over the business. Tell me where I'm wrong."

"If you precede to chase after this elusive white rabbit, I will have no alternative but to call my attorney."

"Officer Thayer, take Mister Shumaker back to his posh hotel." Charlie stood and walked to the door. When he reached the door, he turned around and pointed a finger at Spanky. "Don't leave town because we're not finished."

Chapter 18

Charlie sat with his elbows on his office desk and his forehead resting in the palms of his hands. He stayed up way after midnight. Ma and Da were entertaining Marian and Jack with tales from his youth. Some of the stories he didn't know they knew about. Charlie guessed it was his two younger sisters who ratted on him and his older brother, Sean. After reliving stories of hood surfing and sky walking, he was surprised he had made it to adulthood.

The alarm clock jolted him awake at five-thirty. After silencing the nagging buzz of the clock, he rolled over for just five minutes of cuddling with his wife. After cracking open an eye to check the time, he noticed the five minutes had eased into thirty. Charlie rolled out of bed leaving behind his snuggle bunny, and then stumbled toward the master bathroom.

When he emerged ten minutes later, showered and dressed, the bed was empty and he could smell the aroma of coffee. Charlie found Marian in the kitchen sitting at the breakfast table as she read the local paper. He refused her offer of bacon and eggs, but instead accepted her compromise of toast and a kiss.

As Charlie sat in his office, he smiled as he thought of her sleepy eyes and the silly grin on her face as she kissed him while the bread was in the toaster. He sighed and spoke to her picture sitting on his desk. "Ah, my fair Marian. If anything ever happened …" The words froze on his tongue as he remembered the piece of evidence found at the crime scene. The misshapen heart made from torn bits of paper.

He pushed away from the desk. Looking around cubicle land, he spotted Officer Thayer at his desk. "Good morning." He saw Thayer about to stand. "Don't get up."

Officer Thayer eased down. "Morning, Chief."

"Are you going over the Quinn and Evans file?"

"Yes, sir. I wanted to go through it one more time before our briefing at eight."

Charlie nodded. "I have the autopsy reports on my desk for Mitch and Candi. Nothing much to get excited about there. Have the fingerprints come back yet?"

"No, sir."

"Hmm." Charlie tugged his earlobe. "I'm going to stop by Stewie and Jenny's office." He glanced at his watch, seven-twenty. "I've got plenty of time. I'll meet you in the war room."

Charlie turned toward the stairwell when he heard his phone ring. He trotted back into his office. "McClung speaking." It was Jenny. "What? Slow down, I can barely understand you."

He heard her inhale deeply. "You know what, just meet me in the war room and bring Stewie. Yes, now."

"Thayer," Charlie called out as he exited his office and headed down the hallway. "War room. Now. Jenny and Stewie found something. Where are Willard and Marshall?"

"Probably in the breakroom, sir."

Charlie turned around and headed toward the stairwell. "I'll get them." As he opened the stairwell door, he yelled at Officer Thayer who was gathering up the files for Mitch Quinn and Candace Evans. "Don't let Stewie make the coffee."

Charlie entered the war room with Da behind him carrying a box of warm scones. Some were slathered with strawberry jam, a few with butter, and most had a combination of strawberry jam and freshly whipped cream.

"A gift from me darlin' wife. Best eat them while they're still warm, boys." Before Da could set down the box, Stewie, Jenny, and Officer Thayer were waiting at the snack table.

Officers Willard and Marshall entered the war room a little out of breath, even though they were both in their twenties. Charlie had made them follow him and Da up the stairwell.

"Who made the coffee?" Charlie asked as he poured a cup.

Jenny's hand shot up from the white pastry box. "I did." She sat at the long table with two scones on a small foam plate, and then licked her fingers free of jam. "Stewie wasn't real happy about it. But orders are orders is what I told him."

Charlie circled his finger in the air. "Sit down as soon as you get your coffee and scones. I want this case wrapped up."

The group sat down quickly.

"Jenny, Stewie," Charlie pointed at each of them, "who's going to report?"

Stewie swiveled his torso to look at Jenny's bulging cheeks. "Well, since my mouth is free, I guess I will."

"To the board." Charlie sat down as Stewie took his place in front of the room.

Stewie studied the scribblings on the whiteboard. "So we know three of our suspects, Andrew, Candi, and Heather, were all born in Mississippi. Andrew is the oldest of the three and Candi and Heather are the same age." He paused. "Now this is where things get interesting. Andrew's father was married to Candi's mother briefly, August to November, nineteen-fifty-six."

Charlie interrupted. "The year before Candi was born."

"Correct." Stewie continued, "Long enough for him to possibly be Candi's father."

"But you don't know that for sure?" Charlie caught the wording of Stewie's sentence.

"No, sir."

"Is Andrew's father still alive?" Charlie desperately wanted to speak with him.

"No, sir, but his mother is. And here is her contact information." Stewie handed Charlie a sheet of paper. "It also has contact information for Heather's grandparents and Candi's mother."

164

Charlie was eager to speak to Andrew's mother. "Thanks. What else do you have? Any chance a local address for Heather?"

"No, sir, but you'll find this interesting. If you open the folder marked, Birth Certificates." Stewie continued to speak as they read through the copies inside. "Thanks to Agent McClung, he was able to get Heather's original birth records. You can see that Candi and Heather have the same mother but not the same fathers. Heather was adopted by the parents of the man listed as her father."

Charlie looked up from the copies. "The father on Candi's certificate states, unknown. Why?"

"That you'll have to ask Candi's mother." Stewie recorded the findings on the whiteboard under each appropriate picture.

"Okay, so now we know the connection between these three. Candi's mother. Is there any connection between Spanky and the mother?" Charlie's headache from yesterday was making a comeback appearance.

"None that I can find, but the interesting thing about the mother is she has been busted several times for prostitution throughout the years after Heather was born."

Charlie rubbed his temple and wondered what Candi had been exposed to as she was growing up with a hooker for a mother. Maybe that's how she ended up a stripper. "Hmm, interesting. Since Spanky's boss is tangled up in prostitution and so was Mitch, maybe, just maybe, there's a link. Hmm."

Officer Thayer spoke up. "So right now we know Andrew, Heather, and Candi all lived in Mississippi. Candi and Heather share a mother.

Andrew and Candi may possibly share a father. And Candi and Miss Delaney shared a lover, Mitch." He shook his head and released a slow whistle. "Some kind of messed up stuff."

Officer Marshall chimed in, "And I wonder if there's a reason why Andrew and Heather ended up at The Primrose at the same time?" You know, since there's a familial connection."

"The big question is did the three of them know they were related?" Charlie tapped his pen on the table. He could see the pieces, but they seemed to be from different puzzles. None of it seemed to explain why and who murdered Mitch. "Still no report on the fingerprints?"

Jenny swallowed a gulp of coffee to wash down the last bite of scone, and then answered, "I received a call from your brother's office at the FBI just before we left to come here. All the prints were identified. The cups Andrew and Spanky drank from had their prints. The knife, unfortunately, only had Miss Delaney's prints. Heather's soda can had no identifiable prints, which is understandable. She's never been arrested, has no driver's license, therefore no prints on file. And we should have the results of the prints on the scissors found in Candi's neck maybe late today or in the morning."

"What about this paper heart?" Charlie held up the picture from the evidence folder. "Anyone have any idea what it means?"

Officer Thayer studied the photograph and mumbled, "Messed up stuff I tell ya."

"Willard, Marshall, which one of you found this?"

Officer Marshall, the newest member of the force, answered, "That would be me. I found it at the base of a tree. Whoever was standing there had a view of the bench. There were a couple of footprints found near it, maybe a size nine sneaker, if I had to guess."

"Were you able to determine where the prints came from?"

The newbie shook his head. "No sir, but again, if I had to guess, I'd say from the restaurant or maybe even the parking lot. I'm sorry, sir. Whoever left them was either lucky or knew what he was doing."

Charlie had a thought as he studied the picture of the misshapen heart. "Was there any print or writing on the other side of the bits of paper?"

Officer Marshall's face flushed. "Sir, I didn't look." He stood. "I'll retrieve it from evidence."

Charlie continued as the team waited for Marshall to return. "So do any of you have anything else to add?"

Everyone sat in silence and stared at the whiteboard or flipped through the folders.

"I think it's something to do with Candi. She seems to be the common denominator."

Officer Thayer spoke. "But I don't think she killed Mitch Quinn, Chief. She was wearing a white dress. She would have been covered in blood. And as far as that goes, none of our suspects had blood on them except for Miss Delaney."

Charlie held up his finger. "Ah, let's get to the autopsy report. Also, pull out the blood spatter photos from the crime scene."

Jenny made a squeamish face as she looked at the bloody scene. "Ugh, as many times as I've seen blood, you would think I'd be used to it by now."

Charlie stood in front of a clean section on the whiteboard, and then stuck up a picture of the fan-shaped blood spatter on the path in front of the bench where Mitch sat. "The person who slit our victim's throat appears to have been an expert. They cut the right carotid artery, nicked the left one, and sliced through the trachea."

He pointed to the picture on the board. "As you can see, the blood squirted from the carotid artery roughly three feet in front of the bench. The majority of the blood went forward, not back. More than likely, only a minuscule amount of the blood would have landed on our killer, if any at all."

Charlie posted a close-up of Mitch's head and neck. "We think this is what happened. Our assassin approached our victim from behind and grabbed the hair on top of our victim's head."

The group agreed as they noted the tuft of hair standing up on Mitch's head.

"Then the assassin yanked his head back hard enough to break the skin at the base of his skull." Charlie posted a close-up of the wound. "Skin, hair, and blood was found on the back of the bench, all belonging to Mitch."

Charlie tilted his head backward, then took his index finger and slowly moved it across his throat as he explained. "Now our killer has the neck fully exposed. They pulled the knife across, nicking the left carotid, slicing through the trachea, and severing the right carotid. After the killer slit the throat, he pushed Mitch's head forward. That's why Mitch appeared to be sleeping." He looked at his team. "Mitch would have been unable to speak and was probably unconscious in less than a minute."

"Our killer was right-handed?" Officer Willard asked.

"No, I'm right-handed. That's why I used my right hand. Doctor Jackson explained to me it's impossible to tell if the killer was left or right-handed."

Officer Willard blurted out, "Then it has to be a man."

"Why?" Jenny bristled.

"A woman wouldn't have the strength to do that," Officer Willard snickered.

"You're such a chauvinist!" Jenny snapped.

Stewie said dryly. "Do not anger her. I once saw her bash open a coconut using only her tape dispenser."

Officer Willard flinched.

Charlie laughed. "With the knife found at the scene, it would have been like slicing through butter. Anyone could have done it."

The war room door opened. Officer Marshall entered with a clear plastic bag. "Here it is and it does appear there is something printed on parts of it."

Charlie looked at the small pieces. "Yeah, you're right. Jenny, Stewie, when we're finished here, take this back to the evidence room. Marshall, go with them. I want you to dust every piece for prints, and then piece it together. And I want every step documented with photos."

Officer Marshall took the bag from Charlie and sat next to Jenny.

"Does anyone have any questions or anything to add?" Charlie looked around the table.

Everyone answered, "No, sir."

"All right then, I've got phone calls to make. Jenny, Stewie, and Marshall, as soon as you find anything let me know."

"Yes, sir." They answered collectively.

Officer Thayer and Willard, come with me to my office. You're going to help me with these calls." Charlie clapped his hands together. "Let's get to it."

The team filed out of the room, leaving Charlie and Da behind.

Charlie looked at his father. "Da, are you going home or are you up to staying?"

"Well, son, I think ya got enough help. I think I'll be going home and see what our women are up to. Maybe take them out for a spot of lunch." Da clamped a hand on Charlie's shoulder as they walked down the hallway.

"Call me when you decide where you're going to have lunch. Maybe I can join you."

"Aye, ya Ma and Marian would love that son. And so would I."

Charlie picked up the phone to call Heather Neeley's grandparents but replaced the receiver when he saw Officer Thayer walk up to his door. He motioned his officer to enter.

"Chief, I thought you'd want to know this right away."

"Have a seat."

Thayer sat on the edge of the chair. "You're not going to believe this, but Candi's mother is missing."

"When? Who told you?"

"Well, the number I had was where she used to live. Her ex-boyfriend still lives there. He said he gave her some money, and then kicked her to the street. The last he'd heard, she was living with a couple of hookers at an extended stay. He gave me the name of the place."

"Why did the boyfriend kick her out?"

"He said he didn't mind her hooking. The money was good, but he didn't want her bringing the Johns to the house. And he caught her one too many times with her legs up in the air on their bed."

Charlie grimaced.

"I called the extended stay. The manager confirmed she lived there, splitting a two-bedroom unit with two other girls. So he connected me to their apartment. I spoke to one of the girls by the name of Honey. She complained that it was about time some cop should call about Susan."

"What did she mean?" Charlie jotted down the name.

"According to Honey, Susan was supposed to meet someone. Said whoever she was meeting was going to pay her a boat load of money, an inheritance or something of the sort." Officer Thayer shrugged. "That was about a month ago. No one has heard from her since."

Charlie looked confused. "Why do they think she's missing? I mean, she could've taken the money and decided to leave town, make a new start somewhere else."

"I asked Honey that. She said because Susan didn't take anything with her and she'd never leave without taking the picture of her famous daughter, Candi."

"Hmm." Charlie rubbed his chin. His stomach growled, and he looked at the clock sitting on his desk. Only ten-thirty. He wondered if there were any scones left. Probably not. "Have you called the local department?"

"Yes, sir. I spoke to a Detective Banks who originally took the call from Honey. I didn't get much from him. According to him, it's one less hooker he'll have to keep off his streets. He did say he asked around at some of the known hangouts for her sort. No one had seen her in a few weeks. One of the working girls he spoke to thought maybe she had gone to Georgia to visit her daughter. Banks said he'd call if anything turned up."

"I guess that's one possibility." Charlie made a note to call Detective Hall about Candi's mother. "Do you know if Willard's been able to contact Andrew's mother?"

"There was no answer at her home, but he did leave a message on her machine. He's in Stewie's office hoping they can track down where she works." Officer Thayer stood to leave. "I'll go check on Willard's progress. While I'm there, I'll see if I can get a picture of Candi's mother, maybe one of her mug shots or driver's license."

"Good idea. You're going to make a fine detective."

Officer Thayer grinned. "Thank you." He shut the office door as he left.

Charlie felt the weight of the investigation pressing on his shoulders. It seemed they were getting nowhere fast. He looked at the paper with Heather's grandparents' phone number, and then dialed the number.

Chapter 19

"Thank you, my fine young man." Spanky looked the waiter over. "Nick, is what you said your name is, right?"

"Yes, sir." The waiter removed the spotless plate that once held a six-ounce filet mignon with a mushroom-Madeira sauce, lemon parmesan green beans, and a perfectly baked potato lost under a mound of butter and sour cream.

"How long have you worked here? You're very proficient."

Without hesitation, Nick replied, "I've been here since the beginning, a little over six years."

"Is that right? Would you consider ever working for anyone else?"

"No, sir. Miss Delaney is the best boss I've ever worked for. She calls me her right arm." Nick pointed toward another waiter. "That's Tony, he was hired the same day as me. He's her left arm."

Spanky chuckled. "Let me guess. You're the right arm because you're right-handed and Tony is the left arm because he's left-handed."

"Yes, sir. Would you like a coffee and dessert? Miss Delaney made cannoli this morning."

The mention of cannoli made Spanky smack his lips and forget about stealing Joan's best employees for his boss. "True Sicilian cannoli made with fresh sheep's milk, dark chocolate bits, and candied citrus peel?"

"But of course. Miss Delaney is a Michelin chef. And she fills the shells only when ordered so they won't get soggy."

The large man rubbed his hands together. "I'll take four. Oh, does she serve them with cherries or pistachios?"

"Your choice, sir."

"Both! I want both and a cup of coffee with cream."

"Very good, sir. I'll put the order in, then I'll return to clear the table."

Looking around the simple, yet elegant, restaurant, Spanky wondered if The Primrose would be an acquirable asset. He spotted Nick heading his way.

"You said Miss Delaney is the chef?" Spanky asked as he watched Nick use a gold scraper to banish crumbs from the linen table cloth.

"Yes, sir."

"I would love to give her my compliments and praise her not only on the exquisite food, but also on the outstanding customer service."

"Thank you, sir. May I give her your name?"

"Yes. Tell her, Myles Shumaker."

Nick stopped to attend to another table before going into the kitchen.

Within a matter of seconds, Joan pushed through the kitchen's double doors carrying a plate with four cannoli. Nick trailed behind her with a small silver tray containing a cup and saucer, steamed milk, and a French press.

Joan placed the dessert in front of Spanky and stood on the opposite side of the table while Nick poured out the coffee, making a jack-o-lantern face in the cream. "Good afternoon, Mister Shumaker. I understand you wanted to express your satisfaction."

"Yes, I haven't had a meal in years that could even mildly compare to this epicurean delight, and the service, ah, pure joy."

"Thank you, we're pleased to hear it. Aren't we, Nick? "

Nick stood silently as he waited for Joan's instructions. "Yes, ma'am."

Joan smiled at Spanky. "Do you require anything else at the moment?"

"Yes, I would love for you to sit so we may chat. I have a few questions about The Primrose."

"I believe I can spare a few minutes." She addressed Nick. "That's all for now. Thank you, Nick." Joan gave the young man a generous smile.

Joan waited until Nick was out of earshot before she sat down. "Well, Myles, it's been a very long time."

"Yes, almost twenty years I believe." He picked up one of the cannoli. "Perfection," Spanky sighed, and then bit into the crispy shell. A drop of the creamy filling clung to the corner of his mouth.

Joan couldn't contain the pleasure she felt as she watched Spanky thoroughly enjoying her pastry. "You like it?"

Spanky's tongue darted out to collect the filling clinging to his bottom lip. "Ecstasy, my dear, pure ecstasy!"

"I guess you're here because of Mitch's early demise."

He nodded as he chewed another healthy bite.

Joan waited patiently for his answer.

"Yes, I was here when it happened. I know you didn't do it."

A small gasp slipped from Joan's mouth. "What do you mean you know I didn't do it?"

He held up the china cup, about to drink. "Just what I said. You weren't the only one out there in the woods. I know. I was waiting outside for Candi, you know, Mitch's current infatuation. I saw things." He sipped the coffee. "And by the way, Candi has joined Mitch in the great beyond."

"She's dead? What happened?"

"I think possibly the same person who so conveniently did away with Mitch ended her young life as well."

"Who did you see out there? Who killed Mitch? Myles, please tell me."

Spanky tasted the coffee. "Is there nothing here that isn't superb?" He set down the cup. "I've always liked that you call me Myles. Why do you do that?"

"I know you're not the most honest man I've ever met, but you were always fair and good to me. I respected you for that."

"My dear, that's because you're a decent, hardworking lady. You never lied or held back information from me." He rested back from the table. "I never understood how you got mixed up with Mitch and all that came with it. But at least you had the good sense to walk away."

Joan shook her head and shrugged. "I was way too young and stupid when I met Mitch. I needed someone to love me, shower me with the attention I never got at home." She looked at Spanky. "My parents weren't bad people. They just lived in their own little world, devoted to each other. I was an afterthought, a mistake they had to maintain."

Spanky scanned the room. "Look at this room. It's filled with admirers for you and your talent."

Joan snorted. "You make it sound like I'm back at Ken's Playhouse."

"Oh, no, no, no. You have a respectable establishment here."

"Ah, now I get it." She grinned and shook her finger at Spanky. "You want a piece of the action, don't you? You're going to withhold who killed Mitch unless I cave."

Spanky feigned surprise. "No, but I like the way you think. I could help you make money hand-over-fist, my dear. I mean, I was shocked to see how low the menu prices are. You could charge twice as much as you do. You have to be in the red."

"You're right. I know you are, but I want everyone to be able to experience this kind of place." Joan leaned back and crossed her arms. "And I'll have you know I'm in the black, just barely, but the ink is black. I don't need the money, but you probably already know that."

"Yes, I've kept up with your adventures, although rather boring." Spanky finished a second cannoli and dusted his hands free of pastry flakes. "You're not worried about losing it all?"

"What? You mean by me going to jail for a murder I didn't commit? I'm innocent and McClung will find the one who did it even without your help."

"You seem confident Detective McClung will prove your innocence."

"I am."

Spanky sighed as he poured another cup of coffee. "Well, truth be known, McClung and I, and that includes McClung senior, have a history. And I've no doubt he's the man to solve the crime. Oh, and by the way, Nick is totally devoted to you."

Joan smirked. "You tried to steal my waiter?"

"It's part of my job. Who are those two?"

Joan looked to where Spanky was pointing. "Don't tell me you tried to steal Andrew and Heather, too."

"No, just curious."

"Why?" Joan paused. "You know, Myles, I don't want to know why. I don't care." Joan stood. "I need to get back to the kitchen."

"Your safe haven, huh?"

"Yeah, it …" She stared at the entrance. "Well, speak of the devil, it's Chief McClung. Would you like for me to bring him and his family over?"

"I'd rather finish my last two cannoli in peace."

Joan giggled. "Too late. He's spotted you."

Charlie strolled toward Spanky's table. "Well, it's a small world. How was the opera?"

"Thrilling. The Fox is the perfect venue and once it's fully restored, the place will be most glorious." Spanky bit the third cannoli in half.

"A reunion, I see."

Joan flushed. "Yes, I haven't seen Myles in twenty years."

Marian stood next to Joan, and then greeted Spanky. "It's a pleasure to see you again, Mister Shumaker."

Spanky stood, extending his hand.

Marian accepted.

"Madam, the pleasure is truly all mine." Spanky murmured as he held Marian's hand between his.

Charlie, Da, and Ma rolled their eyes.

"Let me get y'all a table. Follow me." Joan led them to a secluded table at the back of the restaurant.

Charlie lagged behind. "Why are you bothering Joan?"

"I'm not. I came here for a fine meal. I only spoke to her to compliment her success. That's all. Now, I'd like to finish my dessert in solitude. Your family is waiting for you."

Charlie leaned toward Spanky's ear. "Stay away from Joan." He raised to look him in the eyes. "I'm watching you." Charlie then joined his family.

Joan introduced the waiters, even though she knew McClung had interviewed both of them about the murder. She wanted to pretend everything was back to normal. "This is Andrew; he'll be your server today. And I hope you don't mind, Heather will be assisting. She's still in training but she's catching on quick."

Andrew stepped aside. "Heather, why don't you take over, and I'll observe."

Marian smiled at Heather who appeared to be nervous. "Hi, we'll be on our best behavior, promise."

Heather grinned, "Thank you, ma'am. May I tell you our specials for the day?"

Charlie walked up, stood beside Joan, then pulled her aside while his family listened to Heather recite the specials. "Is Spanky bothering you? He said he was here for a meal, but what is he really up to?"

Joan glanced over her shoulder toward Spanky. He was gone. She sighed, "It appears he was here for a few things, one the food, two he tried to lure away Nick, three he wants The Primrose which leads to the fourth reason. He said he thinks he knows who killed Mitch and possibly Candi."

"What? That fat son-of-a ..." Charlie lowered his voice when he saw his mother's look of disapproval.

"He's holding that information hostage in the hope I'll give him my restaurant to avoid jail. Pff! I told him you'd find the murderer without his help." Joan looked anxiously at Charlie. "Right?"

"You know I will." Charlie tugged his earlobe. "And thanks for the compliment."

"Son!" Ma commanded softly. "This is family time."

He felt his cheeks warm at Ma's tone, a tone he grew up with that meant do what I say or suffer the consequences. "Sorry, I need to sit down. But just so you'll know, I'll go speak with him at his hotel."

Joan smirked. "The Georgian? That's where he'd stay back in the day."

"Yeah." Charlie could feel his mother's stare. "We'll talk later."

Marian giggled as her husband sat beside her. "I'm going to have to take lessons from Ma."

Heather stood poised to take Charlie's order. "Would you like to hear the specials, sir?"

"Specials? No, I'll have spinach ravioli on a bed of penne with just a hint of marinara and lots of parmesan." Charlie didn't want to waste any more time. "And I just want water with lemon to drink. Thanks." He watched Andrew and Heather walk away, heads together, their words were hushed.

"Son, ya Ma was asking ya a question."

Da's strong voice brought him from police mode back to family mode.

"I'm sorry Ma. What do you need?"

Ma clicked her tongue. "I want ya to say grace."

Charlie reached for Marian's hand, closed his eyes, and then prayed.

Chapter 20

Charlie hurried into the station. Lunch had taken longer than he had planned. He enjoyed being with Marian and his parents and didn't want to leave them, but he had a job to do. The sooner he solved Mitch's murder, the sooner he could get back to a normal schedule. In his heart, retirement couldn't come soon enough. All he wanted to do was to spend all of his time with Marian.

"Chief, got a message for you." Penny waved a pink square piece of paper. She slid the message through the tray under the bullet proof glass.

He read the name written on the paper. "Yes! You're the best. Thanks."

Penny blushed on cue.

Charlie flashed his name badge at the security pad, and pushed open the heavy metal door as soon as he heard the click. He raced down the hall, up the back stairwell, and into his office.

Charlie was about to shut the door when he heard Officer Thayer.

"Hey, chief! Willard and I got call backs." Thayer made a beeline to Charlie's office.

Charlie could see from the man's expression, he was about to split a gut he was so excited. "Yeah. So did I." He waved the pink slip of paper in the air. "Give me thirty minutes, and then get everyone in the war room. I'll meet y'all there."

Officer Thayer gave him a quick salute. "Sure thing." He headed toward the stairwell.

"Hey!" Charlie yelled at the officer. "Don't let—."

Thayer finished his sentence, "Stewie make the coffee."

"You're a good man, Thayer, a good man." Charlie closed his door. He sat at his desk, pulled out a yellow legal pad, two pens, and then took a deep breath, exhaling slowly.

After dialing the number, he counted the rings. On the fifth ring, the voice of an older woman said, "Hello."

"Missus Neeley, this is Chief Charlie McClung with the Lyman County police department. I hope you're doing well today."

Charlie tapped the legal pad with his pen as Heather's grandmother relived the day's events. "Well, I'm sorry to hear your husband, Hustis, is being a pill today. I'm sure his caregiver understands, but you got a good report from your doctor, right?"

He made a note of her husband's name and the caregiver's while she agreed. "Missus Neeley—."

She interrupted.

"Yes, I'll call you Martha only if you call me Charlie."

She agreed.

"Well, Martha, I have a few questions concerning your granddaughter, Heather." Charlie scribbled as fast as he could. Martha

Neeley had a lot to tell and was eager to share the life story of Heather, her low-life mother, and her weird father.

Forty-five minutes later, Charlie jogged into the war room buzzing with conversation. "Sorry, guys, but Heather's grandmother gave me loads of information." He stood at the whiteboard ready to add to the montage of writing. "Okay, Officer Willard, let's hear what you got from Andrew's mother."

"Her name is Hillary Amanda Johnston. She verified her husband, Ronald, divorced her to marry Susan, Candi's mother. Andrew was five-years old at the time. Ronald and Susan were only married three months before he divorced Susan. And as Missus Johnston put it, 'he came crawling back with his tail between his legs, begging for forgiveness.' She took him back with strict conditions. They remarried and were happily married until Ronald died from prostate cancer two years later."

Charlie interrupted Willard. "Why did Ronald divorce Susan after three months?

"According to her, Ronald found out Susan was a lying whore. She was pregnant before they got married. Ronald swore he didn't have sex with her until their wedding night."

Charlie laughed. "And she believed him?"

"Yep, said that was how Susan got him to marry her." Officer Willard read from his notes. "And I quote, 'The woman, who should have a bright-red letter A tattooed on her forehead, used her wily charms, teased him like Anne Boleyn did Henry the eighth.' End of quote." Willard looked up from his notes. "As Missus Johnston put it, 'the trollop wouldn't spread her legs until there was a ring on her finger.' And once Ronald found out Susan was carrying another man's baby, he left her. He refused to raise another man's mistake."

There were a few laughs and snorts in the room.

Jenny asked, "Did Andrew know about all of this?"

Officer Willard grinned. "Now here's the kicker. About a month ago, someone called Andrew and told him his Daddy had a bastard child. He in turn, bee-lined it home to see his mother. She told her son what he was told was a lie, and then gave him the whole truth. Hillary Johnston didn't give him any names and he didn't ask for any."

"Huh?" Jenny pushed her frizzy red hair behind her ears. "So someone calls, out of the blue after all these years, just to tell Andrew his father cheated on his mother?"

"Yes."

Charlie scribbled the information under Andrew's picture, and then asked, "Was it a man or woman who called him?"

Officer Willard double checked his notes. "A woman, didn't give a name or say how she knew. All the caller said was, 'your father was a lying cheat and has a bastard daughter.'"

"Ah, so the woman was talking about Candi being the bastard daughter. It had to be." Charlie paced in front of the room. "Did you say the caller hung up, didn't wait for a response?"

"Yes, just blurted it out and hung up. But I'm not finished." Officer Willard added. "Andrew's mother said she spoke with her son just yesterday. He told her he had met a woman and she was in deep trouble and he'd do anything to help her get out of it."

"I don't guess we could be fortunate enough to have the woman's name and why she's in trouble?"

Willard frowned. "No, sir. Andrew claimed he didn't want to get her involved. Said it was bad stuff."

"Interesting. Hmm. So we can suppose the woman is Joan, maybe? But the female caller couldn't be Joan, but it could have been Candi or her mother, Susan." Charlie wrote it on the whiteboard.

"Chief, you need to write *deceased* under the name, Susan. That's what I wanted to tell you. Detective Banks called. Susan Evans was found murdered."

"What?" Charlie yelled.

"Sorry, sir, I guess in hindsight, I should have asked to speak first."

Charlie blinked a few times as he stared at Officer Thayer. His mind raced as he stood in silence, and then shook his head. "That's all right. In the long run, it doesn't matter, but we now have one more piece to this ever changing puzzle." He dragged a chair to the front of the room and sat down. "Give us the skinny."

"Detective Banks called me from the scene. Susan Jane Evans' body was found in the woods behind a convenience store a few blocks from the hotel where she lived. The owner of the store found her body after customers kept complaining about the smell coming from his dumpsters."

Charlie glanced at the floor. "Not the dumpsters, but Susan." He looked at Thayer. "How long do they think she's been dead?"

"The coroner thinks maybe a month, but will have a better estimate after the autopsy. Detective Banks thinks she was murdered the night she disappeared."

"Makes sense." Charlie was almost afraid to ask his next question. "How was she killed?"

"Her throat was cut, almost decapitated."

"Oh, gross." Jenny blurted.

Charlie rubbed the end of his nose. "I think we may have a serial killer." He stood. "Which I think rules out Joan Delaney."

"Wait chief." Stewie piped up.

"I'm not going to like this am I?" Charlie squeezed the bridge of his nose with his thumb and index finger.

"Don't forget, only Miss Delaney's prints were found on the knife used to kill Mitch."

Jenny groaned. "The killer could have worn gloves, Stewie."

"Perhaps." Stewie agreed. "Which would make sense. I got the results back on the scissors. Only Candi's prints were found."

Losing his patience, Charlie looked up at the corner of the ceiling and sighed. It seemed as if the investigation was chasing its own tail. He wanted to be home with his wife and parents. He wanted it all over and Joan found innocent. He didn't want to be a horrible boss and scream sarcastic remarks, even though the words were clinging to his tongue waiting to jump off. His staff was blameless, doing all they could, working tirelessly to solve these crimes, but he still wanted to scream.

"Stewie, what else do you have?" Charlie asked softly.

"The only prints found on the scissors belonged to Candace Marie Evans. On the wall safe, not only were Candi's prints found, but Mitchel Daniel Quinn's, and Myles Ely Shumaker's. Numerous prints were found on the door. The ones that have been identified are from employees of the club. Lots of partials found."

Charlie held his breath as he waited for Stewie to get to the bits of paper found at the crime scene.

"The bits of paper found at the scene only had a few smudges no viable prints, nothing of use. But," Stewie held up his long, skinny index finger, "I was able to piece together enough of the paper to determine it's letterhead from the Hyatt Regency."

Officer Thayer added. "That's not too far from the Georgian where Spanky is staying."

"Anything else?" Charlie was disappointed prints weren't found on the paper.

"I called the Hyatt. There is no way of knowing were the paper came from. Not only is it at the front desk, it's in every guest room and office in the building. I did ask if anyone by the name of Andrew Johnston, Heather Neeley, Myles Shumaker, or Candace Evans had ever stayed at the hotel. The answer was no on everyone." Stewie glanced at the file in front of him. "That's all I have to report for now, chief."

"Okay, well, I guess it's my turn." Charlie started pacing, again. "According to Martha Neely, Heather's grandmother, Susan Jane Evans, and her son, William Todd Neely, are Heather's parents. Martha and her husband, Hustis, adopted Heather after Susan Evans … now get this … came over on Christmas day with a four-day old baby girl, shoved a pink bundle into Martha's arms and said 'Merry Christmas,' and then walked away."

"What a horrible woman!" Jenny choked back a sob as she thought of her own little girl. "What about Heather's father? What did he think about it?"

"Martha said her son is a no account alcoholic. She said the only thing her son is good for is hunting, fishing, and drinking, and he's damn good at all of them. She said Heather adores her father and he calls her, his little buddy. When Heather was old enough, he would take her with him on all of his hunting and fishing trips." Charlie paused to get a cup of coffee.

"Don't worry, chief, I made the coffee," Jenny assured.

"Tastes like water if you ask me." Stewie complained.

Jenny punched him on his bony shoulder.

"Police brutality," Stewie said dryly as he massaged his diminutive muscle.

Jenny rolled her eyes. "What else did Heather's grandmother say?"

"Heather knew the story of how Susan had abandoned her on Christmas Day. Martha said Heather made up stories about her mother. She would tell people her mother died from cancer. And Heather also knew she had a half-sister named Candi, but as far as Martha knows, the two have never met. Martha claimed she never told Heather where Susan and Candi lived, only told her their names and no other facts besides they were both worthless whores."

Officer Thayer raised his hand. "Does Heather have a baby and does her father live here, in this county?"

"Good question. No, Heather uses the imaginary baby to get out of trouble or con people into feeling sorry for her. And yes, her father does live in Georgia, but I don't know exactly where." Charlie threw up his hands.

"Martha said only Heather knows where he lives and her son is not married nor involved with anyone that she knows of. So it appears that Heather also lied about a stepmother. Martha said her son has gone a bit squirrely. He thinks there's some kind of conspiracy going on, and he needs to be off the grid. Martha thinks the alcohol has pickled her son's brains."

"I'm guessing Heather's ex-boyfriend is make believe as well." Officer Thayer asked.

Charlie sat down. "Not exactly. He does exist, but he's never been her boyfriend, per se. They attended school together. He joined the army right after high school and was shipped off to South Korea. As far as Martha knows, they haven't been in touch since. That's been about seven years ago." He looked at his watch, almost three-thirty. "Any questions? Anything to add?"

Everyone shook their head.

"Okay, give me theories. Tell me who you think did these murders and why. Did one person commit all three murders or is this just a huge coincidence?"

Stewie replied. "It appears the murders are just a fluke based on the evidence, Joan Delaney killed Mitch, some pissed-off John killed Susan Evans, and Candi ...hmm ... Myles Shumaker."

"I could possibly accept that, but I don't. Why would Spanky kill Candi? Now that Mitch is dead, Spanky will take over Ken's Playhouse. So why kill his money maker?" Charlie stretched out his legs and crossed his arms over his chest, as he waited for Stewie's answer.

Jenny snickered.

"I see your point. Maybe Spanky wanted someone younger and fresher to take Candi's place and Candi refused to get out of the way?"

Charlie bobbed his head side to side. "Yeah, but why try to fix something that's not broke?"

Stewie didn't try to challenge Charlie again.

"Anyone else?" Charlie looked at each blank face. "No? Well, I think I'm this close to solving the case." He held his index finger and thumb apart by an eighth of an inch. "There are still a couple of things I need to find out and verify."

"Chief, we're happy to help any way we can." Officer Thayer offered.

"Thanks. I only have a few calls to make. Thayer, I'll need you to come with me to help find Spanky. I'm hoping he'll be at Ken's or his hotel. I've got a few more questions for him." Charlie stood. "Good work people. I couldn't do my job without your support. We make a great team."

♣♣♣♣

Charlie shut his office door. He sat at his desk and readied for the call to Andrew's mother.

Hillary Johnston picked up the phone on the third ring. Charlie released a sigh of relief, not aware he had been holding his breath.

"Missus Johnston, my name is Chief Charlie McClung with the Lyman County Police Department. How are you today?"

He was surprised at how young she sounded. "Yes ma'am, I doing fine as well. I know Officer Thayer spoke to you earlier today about your son, but I have a few follow-up questions. That is, if you have time."

She quickly agreed.

"If at any time you don't want to answer a question, please tell me. I certainly don't want to cause you any stress.'

Charlie chuckled when she said her life was like an open book that read like *Peyton Place*. "Did Andrew and his father have a good relationship?"

He nodded as Hillary described their relationship, similar to his and Da.

"So your husband took him fishing but not hunting. Did Andrew own a knife?" Charlie scribbled down the types of knives Andrew owned, *Swiss army knife, a small Buck knife, and a folding bait knife.*

"Was the bait knife strictly for bait or could it be used for fileting?" Charlie wrote the word *both*, and then circled it.

He thought of the black dress slacks that all of the wait staff wear at The Primrose. "Could either the Buck knife or the bait knife fit in, say the front pocket of a pair of dress pants?" He wrote, *bait knife in pocket*, then underlined it several times.

"Just one last question. Does Andrew carry the Swiss army knife at all times?" Charlie jotted down, *yes*. "I'm sorry, one more question. Does he ever carry the bait knife with him besides when he fishes?" He made several question marks.

"Thank you, Miss Johnston, you've been very helpful. I hope you have a lovely week. Good bye."

Next, Charlie dialed The Primrose and spoke with Joan about Andrew and Heather's work schedule.

He made one more call to his brother, Sean, at the FBI. Charlie wanted to know more about the fingerprints.

After the call ended, Charlie sat still for a few minutes as he stared at the information Sean, Joan, and Hillary Johnston had revealed. He stood and closed the blinds, shutting out the activity in the cubicles outside his office. Charlie eased behind his desk. He needed to clear his mind and concentrate on the facts of the case.

Charlie closed his eyes, tented his fingers, and then rested his face on them, his thumbs supporting his chin. The suspects and the facts rolled through his mind like a motion picture.

Chapter 21

Officer Thayer drove the squad car down the expressway toward Atlanta. "Chief, you know who did it don't you?"

"Yes, but I can't quite figure out why. I don't want to say who and cloud your judgement. I could be wrong and we need to keep our minds open. We've got to make sure all the pieces are where they belong before we make the arrest."

"It's not Miss Delaney is it?"

Charlie shook his head. "No, I never really thought she murdered Mitch. It was too neat and tidy to put the blame on her."

"But what about the fingerprints? I mean, hers were the only ones on the knife. And it was her knife."

"Anyone could have gotten the knife out of the kitchen and there are plenty of latex gloves laying around the kitchen."

"Hmm, you're thinking someone like Heather or Andrew."

"Yes, but as far as that goes, it could have been Candi or Spanky. Remember, the kitchen has a back door. We have to consider all possibilities. You never know, we could be looking for two murderers."

Officer Thayer stared at the road ahead. "All right, we'll stew on the facts for a while."

Charlie chuckled. "Look beyond the facts. Sometimes you have to look past the obvious. Considering there are, in some cases, more than one way of interpreting the facts."

"More riddles. That makes it as clear as mud."

Charlie smiled at his officer's youth and inexperience. His mind went to the past as they drove in silence to Ken's Playhouse in search of Spanky. The first time he drove down this stretch of highway was the night he met Marian. The night her neighbor, Diane Panell, was murdered. It was also the night he met his friend Jack Jackson, then the assistant medical examiner who performed Diane's autopsy. Without Jack's expertise and honesty, Diane's death would have been ruled a suicide, instead of murder.

Officer Thayer exited the expressway and traveled down Stewart Avenue toward Ken's Playhouse.

Charlie stared at the run-down homes, bars, pawn shops, and one-hour-motels as they passed by, and wondered why nice, quiet areas ended up like this. It was as if neighborhoods just stopped caring and gave up.

They turned into Ken's parking lot. Officer Thayer shifted the car into park. "Well, chief, here we go again."

"Remember, the girls will be working this time. Try not to stare. Okay?"

Officer Thayer held back a grin. "I'm just flesh and blood, sir."

"Well, keep the blood in your brain."

The bouncer let them pass without any questions. Charlie had spoken to him yesterday while they were asking about Candi's murder.

The music was loud and the air was thick with cigarette smoke. The smell of cheap perfume, sweat, and odors of no-telling-what else mingled in the room.

Charlie headed straight to the bar. Luckily it was the same bartender from yesterday. "Is Spanky around?"

The heavily tattooed man shook his head. "No, you just missed him. His taxi left about ten, fifteen minutes ago. He said he was heading back to his hotel, but would be back around midnight."

"Thanks." Charlie handed him a ten dollar bill.

The bartender smiled. "What can I get you? It's on the house."

Charlie waved him away. "Thanks. On duty. Maybe another time." He knew, or at least hoped, there'd never be another time. He looked around the room. All eyes were fixed on the stage, most of the patrons were oblivious to their presence.

There were three gold-colored poles mounted on the stage, with three practically naked young girls entwined around the heavily smudged poles. The look of oh-baby-I've-got-to have-you was fixed on their painted faces, but their glazed eyes said otherwise. The men salivating near the stage only saw their naked gyrations without any thought as to what the girls were really feeling.

"Hey!" The bartender yelled at Charlie. "I don't know if this is important or not, but there was a man in here about five minutes ago looking for Spanky. He wasn't a cop or private dick."

"How do you know?"

"An ex-con knows an ex-con when they see one. And that boy was an ex-con."

"What did you tell him?"

The bartender pulled back his head with a look of confusion. "I told him he wasn't here. What else would I tell him?"

Charlie huffed. "Did you tell him where Spanky was heading?"

"Please, do you think I fell off the turnip truck yesterday? I know who butters my bread. No, I didn't tell the little squirt anything."

"Thayer, hand me …" Charlie punched the ogling officer in the shoulder. "Hey, eyes this way. We're on duty."

Officer Thayer turned red. "Yes, sir."

"Hand me the pictures of our suspects."

From his breast coat pocket, Thayer pulled out four snapshots.

Charlie found Andrew Johnston's photo, then showed it to the bartender. "Is this the guy?"

"Yep, that's him."

"Thanks. You've been a tremendous help." He patted the bar a few times. "I didn't mean to insult, man. Just needed to make sure."

The bartender waved him away. "Think nothing of it."

Charlie handed the photos to Thayer. "Let's go to The Georgian."

Traffic was light. It took Officer Thayer only twenty minutes to get to The Georgian Terrace. He drove into the parking deck and as he pulled out the parking ticket, Thayer complained, "Can you believe this? They charge three dollars an hour for parking. That's highway robbery."

"I'm sure I can convince them to validate it for us." Charlie took the small ticket and shoved it in his shirt pocket.

They walked out onto the sidewalk around to the front of the hotel.

"Impressive. It looks old." Charlie regarded the front of the ten-story hotel. It was built with a buttery-colored brick, marble, and limestone. He turned around and looked across the street toward the Moorish designs of the Fox Theater. The marquee was lit, proudly announcing Giuseppe Verdi's *Rigoletto*.

Charlie pointed to the marquee.

"I guess Spanky was telling the truth." Officer Thayer replied.

"That or just a convenient alibi."

"That's true. I guess we should ask him to show us his ticket stub and program."

Charlie smiled. He knew Spanky could get a stub and program without attending. "Yeah, we'll have to do that." He sighed. "These are very impressive structures. I'll have to bring Marian up here one night."

"Yes, sir. The hotel is the Southern interpretation of a Parisian hotel. It opened its doors in 1911. There's been tons of famous people who've stayed here, movie stars, politicians, rock stars." Officer Thayer stood with his fists resting on his gun belt as he stared with respect at The Georgian Terrace Hotel. Then he turned and gawked at The Fox. "Don't get me started on the Fox. The history and decor of both of these magnificent buildings are indescribable. You have to experience them for yourself."

Charlie patted Thayer on his shoulder. "I'm impressed with your pride and knowledge of history."

Officer Thayer's grin was lop-sided. "Thank you."

"Let's go inside and find Spanky. While we're in there, we'll take a look around."

As they walked up the steps to enter the hotel, Charlie wondered aloud. "Do you think they give tours of The Fox?"

"Yes, sir, I believe they do."

"Excellent."

The white-gloved doorman at the Georgian opened one of the French doors. "Good afternoon."

"Thank you." Charlie and Thayer replied.

White marble columns, Italian-tiled floors, twinkling crystal and bronze chandeliers, and ornate pilasters stunned Charlie as they walked toward the check-in counter.

A young woman smartly dressed, greeted him warmly. "Good afternoon, sir. How may I serve you today?"

"Good afternoon. I'm Chief Charlie McClung with the Lyman County police. May I speak with your manager?" He let the young woman look over his badge.

She smiled, displaying perfect teeth. "I'll be just a moment."

While he waited, Charlie examined the proudly displayed pictures of some of the hotel's famous guests. He stopped at the pictures of

Clark Gable and Vivian Leigh, and thought he'd have to bring Ma to see these, *Gone with the Wind* was one of her favorite movies.

Charlie's walk down memory lane was interrupted.

"Good afternoon, gentlemen. I am Alfred Meadows. How may I be of service?" The salt and pepper haired man extended his manicured hand.

Charlie smiled. "Thank you. I'm Chief McClung and this is Officer Thayer. We need to ask you a question or two concerning one of your guests."

"Shall we go to my office, yes?"

Charlie thought he must be in the wrong business as the manager dressed in a double-breasted, dark blue power suit, thin silk tie, and Italian leather wingtip shoes guided them to his office.

As he sat in the plush leather chair, Charlie wondered what kind of salary Alfred was taking home. "We won't be taking up much of your time. We are investigating a murder." Charlie saw no reaction in Alfred's expression, except for a minute arch of his left eyebrow. "One of your guests, Myles Ely Shumaker, may have some important information that could possibly help solve our case."

"I see. Mister Shumaker has been a guest of ours for many years. A very honorable man."

Charlie held back his urge to laugh hysterically. "Yes, sir. I have known Mister Shumaker for a number of years as well."

This time, Alfred's left eyebrow had a distinct arch. "Well, may I presume you would like his suite number?"

"Yes, sir, that would be helpful."

Alfred reached for an ornate French Victorian style telephone.

"Mister Meadows, if you don't mind, we would like not to be announced."

Alfred Meadows considered Charlie's request. "It is not protocol, but considering you are officers of the law, I am willing to make an exception. But I must insist a bellhop escort you to his suite."

Charlie nodded. "Agreed. Thank you for understanding."

The manager picked up the receiver and dialed. "Miss Smith, please have William come to my office. Thank you."

Alfred shifted in his comfortable chair. "I do hope Mister Shumaker is not in any trouble."

"No, sir, not at all." Charlie recognized Alfred's concern as fishing for information.

A tight little smile pulled at Alfred's thin lips. "I see. That is comforting."

A light rap on the door ended the uncomfortable tension in the lavish office.

"You may enter."

William, the bellhop, entered silently and stood at attention as he waited for instructions.

"William, please escort these two gentlemen to Mister Shumaker's suite. And please wait outside of the suite to escort them back to the lobby."

"Yes, Mister Meadows." With a slight bend at the waist, William held open the heavy wooden door and he waved his hand toward the lobby. "This way."

Charlie and Thayer stood, both thanking Alfred for his assistance.

Once they were all in the lobby, William said, "My name is William, anything you need, you can count on me."

"That's good to know. You can call me McClung and this is Officer Thayer."

"My pleasure to meet you. Do you prefer the stairs," he pointed toward the elliptical staircase, "or the elevator?"

"Which floor is Mister Shumaker's suite?" Charlie loved taking stairs but wasn't up to ten flights.

"Second floor. His suite faces The Fox. He enjoys observing patrons of the theater."

"I bet he does." Charlie snorted. "We'll take the staircase. I've never had the challenge of a staircase like this. Is that okay with you Officer Thayer?"

"I'm willing."

William led the way. "I know you're a policeman obviously by your uniform." He looked at Charlie dressed in a suit. "Are you one too?"

"Yes. I'm acting chief of police. I haven't worn a uniform in years. I've been a detective most of my career. Don't think I'll ever go back to wearing a uniform."

"Cool."

Since William had started the conversation about jobs, Charlie decided to take advantage of it. "William, how long have you worked here?"

"Not as long as Mister Meadows or some of the other staff. I've only been here for eight years."

Charlie was impressed. Nowadays it was hard to find young people who stayed in one job for very long. "You must like the job."

"Yes, sir." The young man answered without hesitation. "I get to meet some pretty famous people and the tips," William whistled softly. "I tell you. I may be just a bellhop, but it's a rewarding job in more ways than one. Yes, sir."

"Did you meet Burt Reynolds?" Officer Thayer's voice was giddy.

Charlie laughed. "Don't tell me you're star-struck?"

"No, well, maybe, it's just he plays such cool parts, tough guy, and funny guy." The excitement in Thayer's voice was obvious.

"Yeah, I did. Had my picture taken with him. He's a pretty nice guy."

"Oh, man! I knew he was a good guy, just knew it."

Charlie chuckled at his officer's joy.

"Almost there." William announced. "Just a few more steps, and then down the hallway. Number 223."

The three men reached the landing for the second floor.

"To the left." William pointed.

Charlie and Thayer followed the bellhop to suite 223.

William knocked on the door. "Mister Shumaker, this is William, the bellhop."

No answer.

The bellhop knocked a little harder.

No sound.

Charlie knew something was wrong.

"Mr. Shumaker!" William banged on the door.

Officer Thayer stepped next to the bellhop. "Are you sure he's in there?"

"Yeah, I saw him come in about an hour ago."

William was about to bang on the door again when Charlie caught his hand. "Wait a minute." He pressed his ear to the door. "I think I hear someone in there." Charlie stepped away from the door.

Thayer and William pressed their ears to the door.

"Yeah, I definitely hear something." Officer Thayer confirmed.

"Me, too." William agreed.

Charlie tried the door knob. Locked. "Can you let us in?"

William nodded. "I've got to run downstairs and get the key." He turned and ran.

Charlie could hear the bellhop pounding down the stairs. He pressed his ear to the door again. "It sounds like Spanky is in trouble." Charlie looked at the lock. "I think I can pick it."

"Wait, I hear William coming up the stairs."

William flew around the corner and came to a sliding stop. Immediately, he shoved the key in the door, turned it, and pushed. William held the door wide open as Charlie and Thayer rushed in.

The room was dark, lit only by the flashing lights from the Fox's marquee that filtered through the crack in the drapes revealing two bodies on the floor, one on top of the other. It was apparent the one on the bottom was Spanky.

Charlie yelled at William. "Call for an ambulance, and then call the police."

"Got it!"

Charlie heard William take off as he knelt beside the bodies. The body on the top was another man. Blood was on Spanky, but it was hard to tell which of the two men was bleeding. Charlie's fingers searched for a pulse for the man on top. "Help me get him off of Spanky."

"Is he alive?"

Charlie nodded. "Just barely."

Thayer positioned his arms to catch the man on top as Charlie rolled him over. The man moaned softly.

"Andrew. It's Andrew." Charlie was confused. It wasn't who he was expecting. Andrews's hands were bleeding. Charlie searched the floor for a weapon. All he saw was blood.

Officer Thayer ran to the bathroom when he saw the blood, and returned with an armload of towels.

"See if you can stop the bleeding while I check Spanky."

Thayer wrapped hand towels around Andrew's hands, and searched his body for more wounds. He found one at the base of his neck, and pressed a white towel on the bleeding wound.

Charlie felt Spanky's wrist for a pulse. It was too difficult to find one under the folds of his neck. "He's alive, pulse is irregular." Next, Charlie examined him for wounds. There were a few shallow wounds on his palms and a couple of scratches on his face.

"They're on the way!" William's voice was accompanied by the sounds of approaching sirens. "What happened?" He flipped on the lights, but stayed glued to the doorway.

Charlie patted Spanky's face. "Hey! Can you hear me? Spanky, answer me. Come on, man, talk to me!"

Spanky's eyelashes fluttered as he groaned.

"That's good, Spanky. Can you talk to me?"

Then Spanky's eyelids flew open and his eyes bulged. "McClung! The boy!" He tried to sit up.

"Calm down. Just lay still. The ambulance is here." Charlie placed his hand on Spanky's broad chest as he easily held him down. The sirens outside the hotel suddenly went silent. The sounds of men running with a gurney across the marble tile echoed up the open staircase.

"The boy." Spanky repeated.

"He's not going to hurt you."

"No, you don't understand." Spanky winced and clutched his chest, smearing blood on his white dress shirt.

Charlie stepped away as the paramedics entered the room.

As the paramedics worked on Spanky and Andrew, Charlie and Officer Thayer searched the rooms.

The bedroom was undisturbed. At the foot of the queen sized bed, laid a silk robe across the thick duvet. Fresh cut flowers in a cut crystal vase graced the center of the mahogany dresser. All the drawers in the two nightstands and dresser were closed.

They moved into the bathroom. Besides being devoid of towels, it appeared to have been recently cleaned and unused. The sink was dry and the faucet sparkled.

"Was there a used towel near the vanity?"

"No, sir. All the towels looked fresh to me, but I was in a hurry."

Charlie heard Detective Hall's voice. "Sounds like the cavalry has arrived."

Detective Hall met them at the bedroom's entrance.

"McClung, we meet again." The Atlanta police detective extended his hand toward Charlie, and then toward Thayer.

"Yeah, looks like my suspects prefer your jurisdiction."

"Both of them?" Detective Hall strolled into the living room. "Looks like this is where it all happened."

Charlie observed the broken lamps, turned over tables, and spilled whiskey.

The paramedics had already taken Andrew out of the suite, and Spanky was being wheeled out as they spoke.

"Hey, are they going to be okay?" Charlie asked the paramedic before he completely disappeared down the hallway.

The hefty man shrugged.

The crime scene unit arrived and invaded the room. They scoured everything in the suite like a hoard of army ants.

William stood at the suite's entrance now joined by Alfred Meadows who held a pale-blue, monogrammed handkerchief to his mouth.

Charlie didn't mean to grin at the manager's delicate constitution. He glanced at Detective Hall.

"Seems like you've got this McClung. Like I said yesterday, I'm just biding my time until the end of the month." He turned his back and stared at the blood spatters.

"Mister Meadows, we'll stop by your office when we're finished. There's nothing here for you to do." Charlie watched him flee toward the elevator.

"What about me? Surely I can be of use." William shifted from foot to foot ready to spring into action.

Charlie didn't want to disappoint the eager bellhop. He rubbed his chin as he considered how William could be of assistance. There were already two Atlanta officers guarding the hallway.

"Why don't you stand at the bottom of the staircase and direct everyone to the elevators? That way if you're needed by the front desk, you'll be available."

"Yes, sir." He grinned and took off.

Detective Hall snorted, "You'd make a fine politician."

"I'm not sure how to take that."

"Let me rephrase that. You'd make an honest diplomat."

"Thank you, I guess."

Detective Hall chuckled. "Let's just say, I'd vote for you. Now, back to business. What did you find when you arrived at the scene?"

Charlie and Officer Thayer took turns describing the scene when they arrived and detailed what had happened since they entered Spanky's suite.

When they finished, Detective Hall slipped a piece of gum into his mouth, working the gum as he chewed on the facts.

Charlie and Officer Thayer declined Hall's offer of gum.

"So, what do you think happened?"

"Well," Charlie massaged the back of his neck, "it appears Andrew came here to talk with Spanky. They argued and fought."

Hall shook his finger in the air. "Yeah, but you don't think that really happened, do you?"

"No. Spanky said 'You don't understand,' when I told him Andrew couldn't hurt him." Charlie paced. "I think there was a third person in this room. The cuts and slashes on Andrew appeared to be defensive wounds. And no weapon has been found."

"Officer Thayer, do you agree with your chief?"

"Yes, sir. I think Andrew stood in front of Spanky protecting him from the attacker. All of Spanky's wounds were superficial; Andrew took the brunt of the attack."

Hall shifted his eyes toward Charlie. "Is that how you see it, too, McClung?"

"Yep."

"Then I guess we need to get to the hospital while my crime scene unit finishes up here."

The three officers descended the staircase in silence. William stood guard at the bottom.

"Thank you, William. I think it's safe for you to go about your regular duties. If you think of anything, anything at all, call me, no matter the time." Charlie handed his card to the young bellhop.

"About that, I think I did see someone. But the thing is, I don't know if it was a man or woman. Or where they went."

"That's okay. Try not to dwell on it. Usually at the weirdest times, the details will pop into your head. When it happens, call me. You got it?"

"Sure thing."

Officer Thayer and Charlie parked at Greater Memorial Hospital. This was the second time for Charlie. The first time was when Diane Panell was brought in. This was where he met Jack. This was where he discovered his boss, Chief Perry Miller, was a dirty cop.

Charlie and Thayer displayed their badges to be allowed to enter the emergency room with their guns. Detective Hall waited for them on the other side of the security check point.

"So what's going on with our two victims?"

"Andrew is in surgery to repair the wound on his neck. He lost a fair amount of blood, but the nurse said he's young and in good shape, so he should be okay. Spanky had a heart attack on the way over here. He's in surgery, too. Him, well, the nurse said we'd have to wait until he's out of surgery."

Charlie tugged his earlobe. "Got any idea when either of them can be questioned?"

Detective Hall threw up his hands and shook his head. "It's just wait and see."

"Damn!" Charlie wanted to stay, but if his suspicions were right, Joan needed to be protected. "I need to make a call. Excuse me."

Charlie walked away. He stopped a passing nurse and asked for a phone. Following the directions, Charlie located the telephone and called his wife.

Marian answered on the second ring.

Charlie loved the sound of her voice. "Hello, darling. How's it going?"

"Hey, Charlie. Where are you?"

"Greater Memorial Hospital. Thayer and I went to see Spanky. We found him lying on his hotel suite's floor with Andrew bleeding on top of him."

Marian gasped. "What happened?"

"We think Andrew shielded Spanky from an attacker. And before you ask me, I don't know why Andrew was in Spanky's room."

"Are they okay?"

"Both of them are in surgery. Andrew should be fine, but Spanky had a heart attack and it's just wait and see for him." Charlie heard her exhale heavily. "Is Da with you?"

"No. He and Ma went to visit the Monastery in Conyers. I was going to go with them, but Haven Place called and needed me to stop by. Da insisted I carry my gun with me because the murderer had not been caught yet. They took my car and I drove Big Willy. I just got back from there."

Charlie groaned. "When will they be back?"

"They said they'd be back in time for dinner. So I guess six o'clock, maybe? Why? What's going on? Tell me."

"Look, I don't want you to panic. Okay?"

"Just tell me, Charlie." Marian's voice was edged with fear.

"I need you to get your gun and have it with you until either Da or I get home. And make sure all the doors and windows are locked and the security system is turned on. Do you know where Joan is?" He could hear Marian walking around the house and was glad they had invested in all cordless phones during the remodel.

"I spoke to her at The Primrose, I don't know, five or so minutes ago. She said she was going home to rest before the dinner crowd showed up. I need to tell her about Andrew. Why do I need my gun?"

Charlie decided to tell her the truth. "I think Heather is our murderer. She's dangerous, hun. My hunch is she's the one who attacked Spanky and Andrew. I don't know who she'll go after next."

Marian grabbed her car keys. "I'm going to her house."

"No! Wait! I'll have a squad car sent to Joan's house." Charlie pulled on his lower lip as he thought. "I'll have a car sent to our house, too."

"Okay, but I don't want Joan to be alone. She's gonna panic when she sees the patrol car in front of her house. You know she will. I want to be there when she arrives."

Charlie rubbed his head. "Fine. If Joan left The Primrose five minutes ago and she drives straight home, she won't be home for at least another twenty minutes. So instead of having a car sent to her house, I'll have just one car sent to pick up you and take you to her house. Wait for the officer to come to the front door. Don't go running out. Once you're inside the car, he'll drive you to Joan's house. And then you wait in the car. In the car, do you understand? In the car with the officer."

"Yes, then what? What do I do when Joan pulls up?"

"You wait for the officer to get out of the car and open your door. In that order, Marian, you don't get out of the car until the officer is by your side. Understand?"

"Uhuh."

"Then you tell Joan to get in the patrol car and both of you go to our house. Stay in the car until the officer clears the house. Then he'll escort you into our house. Once inside, turn on the alarm. The officer will stay posted outside the house."

"Okay, when will you be home?"

"I'm as good as gone. I love you, Marian."

"I love you, too. Please be careful."

Charlie heard the worry in her tone. "You better know it. Stay safe. I'll be there soon. Bye."

"Bye."

Charlie hung up and immediately called the station. He gave them his orders and added a car with two officers to go to The Primrose as well just in case Joan was still there or if Heather decided to show up for work. He wanted one officer inside the restaurant and one patrolling the outside. With all the vulnerable spots covered, Charlie returned to where Detective Hall and Officer Thayer were standing.

"Anything new?" Charlie asked.

"No, one of the nurses just reported it could be awhile. She said we were welcome to stay or she'd call us as soon as either one of them is able to talk." Detective Hall took off his hat and fanned his face. "Is it hot in here?"

Charlie and Thayer both answered, "No."

"My wife thinks it's my thyroid." Hall hunched up his shoulders. "Who knows? Anyway, I don't think there's any reason for us to be hanging around the hospital."

"Yeah, you're right, I'd really like to get home and check on things there." Charlie was relieved knowing he'd be with Marian soon.

Hall continued fanning himself, beads of sweat dotted his forehead and upper lip. "Sounds good. How long will it take you to get back here from your house?"

"Thayer, how fast can you get us back here from my house?"

The young officer grinned. "With the lights and siren on, I'd say twenty minutes, fifteen if the traffic isn't too bad."

"Here's another one of my cards. Call me as soon as you hear anything."

"Thanks. I left the other one on my desk." Detective Hall removed a thin bi-fold wallet from inside his trench coat, and inserted Charlie's card. "I'll call you as soon as I get word."

Charlie turned to leave, stopped, and snapped his fingers. "Thayer give me Heather's picture."

"You think she's the murderer?" Thayer handed Charlie the photograph.

"Bingo." Charlie turned. "Hey, Hall. This is who you should be looking for."

Hall looked at Heather's young sad face. "You've got to be kidding me. Her?"

"Don't let her baby face fool you. Her name is Heather Morana Neeley and she's twenty-five years old. We think she killed her own mother, Mitch Quinn, and Candi Evans, who happened to be her half-sister."

Detective Hall grimaced. "Been in this business for over forty years, you'd think by now nothing could surprise me.

Chapter 22

Marian sat in the living room with her legs and arms crossed as she waited impatiently for the officer to arrive. Her top leg swung nervously. She stood and marched toward the phone, picked it up, and then dialed Joan's home number. No answer.

The doorbell rang.

"Missus McClung! This is Officer Willard. Chief McClung sent me."

Marian squinted her left eye as she put her right eye against the peephole to verify he was who he said he was. "All right. I'll be out in just a second."

She turned off the alarm and reset it, grabbed her purse, tucked her pistol inside, patted her front pants pocket for Joan's house key, and then opened the front door.

"Good afternoon, ma'am, I'm to take you to Miss Delaney's house." Willard touched the brim of his hat and dipped his head.

"Yes. Charlie's given me strict instructions. It's good to see you, again, but I wish it were under less stressful circumstances."

"Yes, ma'am."

As they walked toward the patrol car, Officer Willard scrutinized the surrounding area, his hand poised on the butt of his revolver. He opened the back passenger door for Marian. Once safely inside the car, he drove around the cul-de-sac and headed for Joan's house, two streets over.

Marian noticed Joan's car was not in the driveway. Joan always parked in the driveway instead of the garage if she knew she wasn't in for the night. But, Marian thought, maybe because of what's going on, she may have parked in the garage. No need to get worried, yet.

Officer Willard pulled into the driveway and parked as close as he could to the front door.

"Please, can you check to see if Joan is home? She should have been home by now."

"Chief McClung instructed me to stay in the car with you."

"But what if she's inside and the killer has her? Please." Marian reached inside her purse. "I'll be fine. I have my pistol with me." She showed Officer Willard her weapon.

He thought about it. "Fine, but don't you set one foot outside of this car. And don't tell the chief I left you alone or he'll have my head on the end of a dull stick."

"Thank you! I promise."

Marian stayed inside the car while Willard knocked on the front door.

Joan didn't open the door.

Willard knocked again and called out to her.

Still no answer.

The officer retreated and opened Marian's door. "Ma'am do you have Miss Delaney's house key?"

Marian had already pulled the key from her pocket. She shoved it into Willard's hand. "Here. Let me come with you."

"No, ma'am. I need to clear the house." He shut the door.

Marian knew she couldn't defy his order and escape from the back of the patrol car. She was a prisoner. Marian kept a watch of what was going on around her and prayed Joan was all right.

Officer Willard emerged from the front door.

Marian couldn't read his blank face. She felt like crying.

He had barely cracked open the driver's door before she began the third degree.

"Is she home? Is she okay? Has she been home? Did someone kidnap her? Tell me, please! What did you find?"

Officer Willard held back his amusement. "No, ma'am. She isn't home and it doesn't appear any harm has come to her. Everything looks in order. I'll call the station. Just relax back there."

Marian felt like screaming, but she held her tongue. Last thing she wanted was for Charlie's men to think she was some out-of-control harpy. Instead, she stared down the road watching for Joan to drive up as she listened carefully to Willard's side of the phone conversation.

Not knowing the whereabouts of Joan, each second of the call was agony for Marian. And Officer Willard keeping an eye on her from the rearview mirror was unnerving. His side of the phone call was devoid of any useful information. Mainly, *yes*, *no*, and *I understand*.

Officer Willard ended the conversation.

"Well, what did you learn? Has Joan been found?"

"So far, we know she is not at home, nor is she at The Primrose. Nick Cusack, the person in charge, reported Miss Delaney left the restaurant about an hour ago."

"An hour ago! She should've been home over thirty minutes ago. She told me she was going home to rest! Did she say where she was going? Did she?"

"He doesn't know where she was going, he assumed home. Miss Delaney informed him she would return around seven o'clock."

Marian glanced at her wristwatch. It was almost six o'clock. Her breath became short and heavy. "Where could she be?" She felt a churning in her stomach as panic tried to gain control over logic. Opening her purse, Marian pulled out a tissue, and then pressed it on the inside corners of her eyes.

A car honked its horn.

Marian jumped at the sound. "It's Joan. Oh, thank God." She tried to open the door. "Let me out, please."

"Hang on. I need to make sure everything is okay before I let you out."

"Hurry." Marian beat the window and waved vigorously to get Joan's attention. "Joan! Are you all right?"

Joan pulled up beside the patrol car and let down her window.

Officer Willard walked up to Joan's car and looked in the back seat. "Miss Delaney, is everything okay?"

"Yeah. Why is Marian in your car?" Joan stared at Marian, and then looked up at the officer. "What's going on?"

"Everything is fine. It's for her own safety."

Joan's mouth fell open. "Safety? From what?" She opened her car door only to have Officer Willard put his hands up to stop her from getting out. "What are you doing? I want to talk to Marian."

"It's for your own safety, ma'am."

"Will you stop saying that and tell me what is going on."

"Yes, ma'am, but you need to come with us."

"But I need to get my clothes for work."

"Fine. Pull into the garage first and once you're safe inside, I'll bring in Missus McClung."

Joan remotely opened the garage, and pulled in as Officer Willard followed her car inside.

Marian watched from inside the locked patrol car as the garage door slowly closed with Joan and Officer Willard inside. She thought, well, Charlie doesn't have to worry about Willard not taking his job to protect and serve seriously.

A few moments later, Willard came out of the front door, and escorted her inside Joan's house.

Marian rushed to Joan and threw her arms around her friend. "Where have you been? I've been worried sick about you."

"I'm sorry. I finished up the fudge last night, so I stopped for ice cream to cheer me up." Joan held Marian back at arm's length. "I had no idea you were looking for me. Officer Willard gave me a shortened version of what's going on."

"I know. It's just—."

"Shush! Don't even start. I'm fine. You're fine. We're all fine. Let me grab a clean chef's uniform and we'll be on our way. I'll get ready at your house."

Marian smiled. The uniform Joan was wearing looked pristine. "What are you going to fix for dinner?"

"For you, the finest peanut butter and jelly sandwich you've ever had."

Marian appreciated Joan making light of the situation and taking to heart her favorite quote, '*Worry is like a rocking chair. It gives you something to do but doesn't get you anywhere.*'

She and Officer Willard followed Joan to her bedroom. Marian went inside with her, while Willard stood guard at the open door.

Marian sat on the king-sized canopy bed while Joan pulled out a few underthings from a chest of drawers, and then flung them on the bed. Marian laughed when she saw a pair of white cotton panties land next to her. Picking them up, she said in disbelief, "Really, Joan? I never figured you for granny panties."

"Those are what I call kitchen drawers. Don't make fun of them. They're most comfortable." Joan walked through the bathroom and into the walk-in closet. She returned carrying a hanger with a uniform under dry cleaner's plastic. "I'm ready to go."

Marian picked up the undergarments. "What are you going to put these in?"

Joan looped the panties, bra, and camisole over the hook of the hanger. "Let's go."

Marian rolled her eyes. "Whatever. By the way, you know you're staying with us until your murderous waitress is found, so make sure you have everything you need for tonight."

"You say it as if it's a bad thing. As long as Ma is cooking and baking, I'm fine with it."

Charlie and Officer Thayer pulled up behind Officer Willard's patrol car parked in Joan's driveway.

"Well, so far, not so good. Willard and Marian were supposed to stay in the car while they waited for Joan to arrive." Charlie mumbled as he emerged from the cruiser. "Wait here, Thayer, and keep a sharp eye out while I go see what's going on inside."

Officer Thayer got out of the car and stood guard.

Charlie's hand was poised to open the front door, as it suddenly flew open.

Officer Willard stood like a statue. "Sorry, chief. I had to disobey your orders. Miss Delaney needed to get some things from the house."

Charlie laughed, relieved all was well. "Good one, Willard. You looked out the peephole and thought you'd surprise your boss and fling open the door, yeah?" He slapped the officer's shoulder. "I'm glad I didn't shoot you." Charlie clicked his tongue and pointed his index finger at Willard.

Officer Willard relaxed, happy to know his head would continue to be attached to his neck and not mounted on a pole.

"Charlie!" Marian pushed aside Officer Willard and threw her arms around her husband.

"I'm guessing Joan is okay."

Joan leaned her head around Marian. "So far, so good." She held up the clothes hanger. A white lacy bra flopped around as she shook the hanger.

Officer Willard groaned at the sight. "Ladies, are you ready to leave?"

"Yes, we are." Marian walked out and waited for Joan to lock the front door, then Charlie and Officer Willard escorted them to the cars.

"Do you mind if I ride with Joan back to our house?"

Charlie kissed Marian's forehead. "Not at all. I'll see you at home. We'll be right behind you all the way."

They all pulled into the McClung's driveway. Marian and Joan waited for Officer Willard to release them from the backseat.

Charlie escorted Marian and Joan into the house while Thayer and Willard did sentry duty outside. When they opened the front door, they smelled the aroma of coffee, and scones, and heard Ma and Da's laughter coming from the kitchen.

"Ma, did you have a good time at the monastery?" Charlie kissed his mother's soft cheek.

Ma embraced her son. "Aye, that we did indeed. I had to make scones for all the jams we bought." She held out her arms. "Come here my loves."

Marian and Joan nestled into Ma's hug.

"Ma, you're going to make me fat." Marian giggled.

"Me, too." Joan agreed.

Da stood in front of the women. "Ah, ya both nothing but skin and bones." He pulled Ma's curvaceous body into his arms. "Now, this is what I call perfection."

The telephone rang, interrupting the moment.

"McClung, here." His smile melted away. "Yeah. An hour you say? All right, we'll be there."

Marian slid her arm around Charlie. "The station?"

"Yeah."

"Are you leaving this minute?"

He shook his head. "No, but we'll have to leave in about thirty minutes to go back to Greater Memorial. Spanky and Andrew are out of recovery and in ICU."

"What happened, son?" Da asked.

"The short version is someone attacked Spanky and Andrew intervened. Thayer and I found them in Spanky's hotel room this afternoon."

Ma poured coffee for everyone. "Are they going to be all right?"

Charlie took the cup his mother offered. "Should be." He sat at the kitchen table. "Andrew had a pretty nasty cut and lost a lot of blood and Spanky had a heart attack."

"I'm going to take this to Thayer and Willard." Marian had two mugs of coffee in her hands.

"No, I'd rather Da take it."

Da nodded. "It's the crazy little girl waitress. She's on the loose."

"When did you figure it out?" Charlie was amazed by his father's deduction.

"After I spoke to ya brother. I put two and two together and got Heather. So I'm right, yeah?"

"That you are. Well, I'm pretty sure. Once we question Andrew and Spanky, we'll be positive." Charlie looked at Joan licking jam off of her fingers. "When you're ready, I'll have Willard drive you to The Primrose. And someone will bring you back."

"Yeah, I know. I'm your guest until Heather is behind bars." Joan washed her hands. "You don't honestly think she'll come after me. What would be her reason?"

"The girl's not right in the head." Charlie finished his coffee. "I'm just playing it safe. And just so you know, there will be an officer outside the kitchen door and one hidden around the entrance, just in case Heather thinks we're not on to her and shows up for work."

Joan grunted. "I know this sounds petty in light of everything, but I'm going to be short two waiters."

"We'll help if you feed us." Marian hooked her arms around Ma and Da's elbows. "Is that okay with y'all?"

"Sounds like a grand idea. It'll be fun!" Ma consented.

Da hiked up his pants leg, exposing an ankle weapon. "I can help with security."

Charlie looked at Joan. "It's your decision. Do you want the Apple Dumpling Gang or not?"

"Do I have a choice? Where can I find help this late? They're better than nothing." Joan grinned. "Besides, they're cheap." She clapped her hands. "Chop, chop! I'll be ready to go in ten minutes."

Chapter 23

Officer Thayer stared at the highway as he drove to the hospital. "So tell me, chief, how did you figure out it was Heather?"

"A couple of things. Heather steered us away from herself as a suspect. For example, she only told Andrew, none of the other staff, about Joan and Mitch's midnight rendezvous. I think because she knew Andrew has a bit of a crush on Joan, Heather counted on Andrew going to Joan's rescue. Also, she cleverly mentioned she witnessed Candi and Spanky together that night. And she never told us Candi was her half-sister. Why?"

"It would make her a suspect for the murder of Candi and possibly their mother."

Charlie nodded. "Right."

"Why kill Mitch and go after Spanky and Andrew?"

"I'll get to that later. Another thing that piqued my curiosity about her were the fingerprints. I called my brother to verify the findings." Charlie braced himself as Thayer made a sudden lane change and flew up an exit ramp. "This is interesting. You're going to love it. The smudges were fingerprints. Heather has no fingerprints."

Officer Thayer's eyes bugged out as he blurted, "What? How?"

"Heather was born without fingerprints. It's a very rare genetic disorder called Adermatoglyphia. And luckily, when she was born, not only did the hospital take footprints, they also took handprints. I compared the birth certificate prints to the prints found on the soda can and verified her disorder. So that explains why only Miss Delaney's fingerprints were found on the murder weapon and Candi's on the scissors. The smudges were Heather's non-fingerprints."

Officer Thayer smirked. "But how could someone as small as Heather overpower Mitch?"

"Remember, Candi said she overheard Mitch say, '*It's about time*'?"

"Yeah."

"And the medical examiner's theory of Mitch being approached from behind before he was killed?"

"Yeah."

"Well, Mitch probably never saw the person. He just assumed it was Joan, never thinking someone else knew of their plans. And I learned from Heather's grandmother something interesting."

"What's that?"

"Heather had a good relationship with her father. She was his hunting and fishing buddy. She knew how to use a knife and how to be very quiet in the woods."

Officer Thayer pulled into the hospital's parking deck. "I see, but I still don't understand why she killed Mitch and Candi."

"Mmm, I have to be honest with you. I can't quite figure out Mitch. Candi? I'll take a guess because Heather was rejected by her mother, when Candi wasn't. And I'll venture to guess, Candi probably rejected her as well."

"Why did she attack Andrew and Spanky?"

Charlie unleashed his seatbelt. "I believe she overheard Joan telling me that Spanky knew who the killer was. Why was Andrew in Spanky's suite? That's another puzzlement. We'll just have to find out from him."

Charlie and Officer Thayer met Detective Hall in the ICU waiting room.

"McClung," Detective Hall glanced at his watch. "You made good time."

Charlie slapped Thayer's back. "This man can drive, a little unnerving at times, but we made it." He shook hands with Hall. "What's the status on Andrew and Spanky?"

"Both resting comfortably. Andrew is more alert. Spanky, well, he's going to need more time, being older and all." Detective Hall pointed to a coffee pot, his Dick Tracy hat next to it. "Do you want a cup? I finished one right before y'all walked in. It's pretty good, but you'll have to drink in here. The nurses chased me out of ICU because I entered with a cup in my hand."

"Nah, I'm ready to question Andrew." Charlie glanced at Thayer. "What about you?"

The officer shook his head. "No, I'm good."

Hall picked up his hat. "Let's go. Oh, by the way, the nurses will let only two of us in the room. One of us will have to stand outside in the hallway."

Officer Thayer sighed heavily. "I'll wait outside."

Detective Hall picked up the telephone hanging on the wall right outside of the ICU locked double-doors. "Detective Hall with Chief McClung to see Andrew Johnston in unit four."

An audible metallic click echoed in the hallway. Hall pushed open one of the doors and held it open for Charlie and Officer Thayer. Just as he was about to release it, a doctor ran up.

"Thanks for holding it open. Sometimes these things don't work." The doctor held up her employee badge.

Hall smiled at the doctor as she passed by, and then watched her walk toward the nurses' station. He caught up with Charlie and Thayer as they rounded the corner toward Andrew's room.

The three men stood outside of his room. Through the wall-sized window, they observed Andrew sleeping.

"He doesn't look that bad, a little pale maybe." Charlie noticed he was breathing on his own, and with only a few tubes in his arms, one for blood, and a couple of bags of clear fluids. "Shall we?"

Charlie and Hall entered Andrew's room as Thayer watched from outside.

Softly, Charlie spoke as he gently squeezed Andrew's cold hand. "Andrew, can you hear me?"

He could see Andrew's eyeballs move under his eyelids, then his lids cracked open. A heavy breath escaped his dry lips. "Yes."

Andrew raised his right hand and rubbed his face. The movement caused the fluid bags to rattle against the metal pole where they hung. "Water." He tried to move his left arm, the one with the tube for the blood, but it was tied down. Andrew groaned.

"Here you go." Charlie held a plastic cup to Andrew's mouth. "It's water. Drink."

Andrew's eyes opened and stared at Charlie as he drank. "Thank you." He raised his head and scanned the room. "Why am I ... oh, I remember." Andrew's head fell back onto his pillow.

"Andrew, do you remember me?"

"Yeah, you're McClung. Who's he?" Andrew nodded toward Hall.

"He's Atlanta police detective Lawrence Hall."

Andrew licked his parched lips. "Makes sense."

Charlie offered Andrew the cup of water.

He took the cup and drank it dry. "Thank you."

Detective Hall spoke. "Do you feel like answering a few questions, son?"

"Yeah."

Hall looked at Charlie and nodded for him to take control.

"Who attacked you?"

Andrew grunted softly. "Heather."

Charlie turned toward Thayer and mouthed Heather's name.

Officer Thayer gave him a thumb's up that he understood.

"Why were you in Spanky's suite?"

"I overheard Miss Delaney tell you Spanky knew who killed Mitch. I don't want her to go to jail for something she didn't do."

"I see. You went to his hotel to make him tell you who did it."

"Yeah."

Charlie refilled the cup with water. "Do you need another sip of water?"

Andrew reached for the cup and held it as he spoke. "When I got to his room the door wasn't shut completely. So I pushed it open, and then …" He grimaced and took a sip. "The room was dark. I think only one lamp was turned on. There stood Heather holding this knife, a hunting knife, I think. Spanky had his hands up in the air. She turned and lunged at me." Andrew's breathing became heavy.

Charlie put his hand on Andrew's shoulder. "Take it easy. Try and keep calm. Okay?"

Andrew drank more water and gave Charlie the empty cup. "We fought as I tried to get the knife away from her. God, she's strong. I remember Spanky tried to help. He fell. And then she …" Andrew touched his neck. "I guess she stabbed me."

"What happened next? Why did she leave you two alive?"

"I remember hearing loud voices in the hallway." Andrew shook his head. "I don't know, maybe she panicked. I don't know."

Charlie heard screaming and crashing sounds. He turned in time to see Officer Thayer take off down the hallway. Charlie ran out of the room and yelled over his shoulder at Detective Hall. "Protect Andrew."

Charlie heard the door slam behind him. The screaming came from Spanky's room down the hall.

When he entered the room, there was a bloodied nurse laying on the floor. Officer Thayer struggled with a woman in a white lab coat. Charlie grabbed for the woman's hand holding a scalpel.

The three of them tripped over the nurse laying at their feet. The crazed woman slashed wildly in the air.

Charlie watched in horror as the scalpel plunged deeply into Thayer's shoulder. Then the woman turned on him. He almost didn't recognize her. But it was Heather. Her freckles were covered with makeup and her eyes were painted like Candi's with eyeshadow and black liner.

She screamed and slashed the blade at him.

Charlie felt a deep sting across his left forearm as his right fist made contact with her cheek.

Heather dropped the scalpel as she fell to the floor, hitting her head on the foot of the bed.

A doctor rushed into the room and quickly attended to Spanky. The doctor was followed by two nurses who attended to Thayer and their fallen co-worker, while Charlie handcuffed an unconscious Heather.

Charlie and Officer Thayer sat on gurneys in the emergency room while the doctors stitched their wounds.

"My wife's not going to be pleased to see this." Charlie motioned toward his left forearm with seven small stitches and counting. "How many more do you think it needs?"

The doctor wobbled his head side to side. "Hmm, probably five or six more. I'm putting them pretty close together so it won't make a huge scar to remind your wife of what could have happened."

"Thanks, you're a good man."

The gray-haired doctor smiled. "Through the years, I've stitched up plenty of cops. I've learned their wives worry enough. They don't need any in-your-face war souvenirs."

The young doctor attending Thayer sat back and inspected his handiwork. Heather not only stabbed him, but turned the blade, then pulled down, and out. "I did the best I could, but the way I had to stitch the wound closed, your scar's going to look kind of like an exploded balloon."

Officer Thayer looked at the needlework. "Hmm, I'll call it a ninja death star."

Charlie watched as a nurse wrapped a bandage around his forearm. His doctor had moved on to the next patient. Charlie made a fist with his left hand, flexed his arm, and winced.

"Your arm will be a little sore and stiff for a few days. The doctor left a prescription for an antibiotic. No telling where that scalpel came from. Just take some ibuprofen for the pain and stiffness. That goes for both of you." She patted Charlie's hand and said over her shoulder, "You're both going to live."

He laughed as he slid his bandaged arm through the blood-soaked, torn sleeve of his white dress shirt. "I can't say that for this shirt. It's a goner."

"Mine looks like I had my heart ripped out of my chest." Officer Thayer observed as he buttoned up his ruined uniform shirt.

"Do you have a spare in the car?" Charlie thought about his clean shirt that hung in his office.

Thayer shook his head. "I will after today."

"Let me call Marian before we go check in on Andrew and Spanky. Then we'll head over to Detective Hall's precinct." Charlie decided he'd wait until Marian saw him alive and kicking, and after he stopped by his office to change shirts, before telling her about the scuffle with Heather and its outcome.

Charlie's nurse pointed toward a wall phone. "You're welcome to use that one."

The emergency room doors burst open with multiple gurneys carrying victims of a serious car accident. The nurses yelled at Charlie and Thayer. "You're good to go, now. We need this space."

They bee-lined it out of the room and made their way back up to the ICU. The charge nurse in the unit gave Charlie permission to use the desk phone. He called The Primrose and spoke to Marian. Her voice sounded happy. Charlie guessed waiting tables was fun for one night, and he bet her feet would need a good soak and rub once she got home. He smiled at the thought of Marian, Ma, and Da sitting in the kitchen with their feet in a big tub of hot Epsom salt water while they ate scones and drank coffee.

Charlie hung up the phone. He spoke to one of the nurses sitting at the desk. "How is Myles Shumaker doing after the incident in his room?"

"In the long run, he'll be okay. The woman didn't have time to do much damage. She managed to pull out his IVs, but his nurse caught her just as she pressed the scalpel to his neck." The nurse shook her head. "The wound on Mister Shumaker's neck didn't require stitches, but Marge needed a few."

"Will Marge be okay?" Charlie was upset that one tiny little girl could inflict such destruction.

"Yeah, she'll be fine." The nurse giggled. "Marge will have one heck of a story to tell."

"Can we speak to him?"

"Sure, if he's awake. You know, he slept through the whole thing."

Charlie grinned. "Huh, imagine that. Thank you for your help. We'll check on Andrew Johnston, too, if it's okay."

"We all want to thank you two for the rescue. No telling what would have happened if you hadn't been here." The nurse shuttered as she rubbed her arms.

"Thank you." Charlie and Officer Thayer replied.

They stopped by Andrew's room first.

"How are you feeling?"

Andrew swallowed a bite of red Jell-O. "What happened out there? They won't tell me nothing, except there was an accident and everything is good. Not to worry."

"Heather paid Spanky a visit."

His mouth fell open. "What? Is he okay? I mean she didn't—?"

Charlie cut off his sentence. "No, she didn't. And don't worry, she can't come after you, either. Heather is locked in jail."

Andrew's head flopped back on his pillow and closed his eyes. "I spent five years in jail and never had anything like this happen to me."

"You're safe. There are guards posted at the entrance of the ICU ward."

Andrew's eyelids popped open. "Why? I thought you said she's locked away."

"Don't worry, she is. We're just being on the cautious side." Charlie looked at the food on the hospital tray. "I think you should be worried more about starving to death."

He chuckled. "You've got a point. I can't wait to get back to The Primrose." A look of panic shadowed Andrew's face. "Miss Delaney, is she okay?"

"Yeah, she's fine." Charlie leaned over and whispered to Andrew. "If you're still in here tomorrow, I'll have one of Miss Delaney's gourmet burgers brought to you."

"You're an evil man tempting me with contraband food, McClung, but I'll owe you one if you do." Andrew licked his lips at the thought of the promised hamburger.

Charlie looked at Thayer. "Write that down." He then stared at Andrew. "We'll need to get your written statement."

"I think if I get that burger, I'll have enough energy to do it. Right now ..." Andrew raised his arm slightly and let it fall. "See, no strength to even sign my name."

Charlie snickered. "We'll see you tomorrow."

They strolled toward Spanky's room. A scowling nurse stormed out of his room carrying a tray.

"Is everything okay?" Charlie held up his hand to stop her.

"He refused to eat this … slop as he called it. Told me to get his doctor or he's suing me and everyone else in this building."

Charlie let the nurse go as he looked at Thayer. "I guess he's awake enough to talk."

"Yeah." Thayer followed Charlie into Spanky's room.

Spanky lay with his eyes closed and spoke without opening them. "Well, that was quick." He looked toward the door. "Oh, it's you, McClung. I guess I owe you a thank you. I understand you've saved my life twice."

"Just doing my job, but you're welcome." Charlie walked closer to the bed. Officer Thayer stood beside him.

Spanky blanched at the sight of their blood-stained clothes. "Good God in heaven. Did the she-devil do that?"

"Yeah but it's not as bad as it looks. Speaking of which, you don't look so bad for someone who was almost murdered two times."

Spanky splayed his fingers. "I guess it's going to take more than a skinny little hellion to kill me."

Charlie saw sweat bead on Spanky's forehead. "Look, you need your rest and I need to question your attacker."

Spanky grunted. "You're too much of a gentleman to call her what she really is."

"Hmm. Well, I need to ask you a question or two before we leave. Did you see Heather kill Mitch?"

"No, but I had my suspicions. I saw her run out of the woods. I didn't think she saw me." Spanky glared at Thayer. "I saw you roll your eyes. What? You don't think a fat man like me can hide?"

Officer Thayer didn't answer as he bit his lips to keep from laughing.

Charlie rubbed the back of his head. "Do you think you'll feel like giving your statement in the morning?"

"Yeah, that is if," Spanky yelled toward the door, "they don't starve me to death!"

Chapter 24

Charlie and Thayer greeted Detective Hall as he stood outside the entrance of his precinct.

Hall tossed a to-go cup in the trash. "Ready?"

"Yes, did she give you any problems?" Charlie walked up the stairs beside Hall with Thayer following behind as they entered the building.

"Nah, she's been unusually quiet. We're holding her in a cell by herself. We didn't want to take a chance she'd go all homicidal on a cell mate."

Detective Hall led them to his desk. "Have a seat. There's coffee over there if you're interested." He pointed to a far corner of the busy room crammed with desks. "I'll have her brought up so we can interview her."

"Thanks." Charlie headed toward the coffee.

"Man, I thought we had it bad." Officer Thayer gawked at the officers' exposed, overcrowded workspace.

Charlie poured a small amount of coffee into a foam cup, and then tasted it. He bobbed his head. "Not bad." He filled up the cup. "I could've told you, you're working in the lap of luxury. This is typical." Charlie waved the cup of coffee around the tight maze of desks. "That's one good thing I can say about Chief Miller, he put some of the profits from his drug running operation to good use. Yep, made sure his command had the best of everything."

"I'll never complain again."

Charlie sipped the coffee as they snaked their way back to Detective Hall's desk.

"They're on their way with her. By the time we get to the interview room, she should be there."

The three men arrived just as two officers sat Heather down and locked her cuffs to the table. "She's all yours. We'll wait outside."

Heather stared at the two-way mirror, never acknowledging Charlie, Hall, or Thayer.

Hall pointed at Charlie and gave him a thumbs up.

Charlie and Hall sat across from Heather while Thayer stood in front of the locked door.

"Hello, Heather, can we get you something to drink?" Charlie asked softly.

Her dead eyes focused on Charlie's face, and said nothing.

All right, Charlie thought, this is going to try my already worn-thin patience. "Heather, you know why you're here, don't you?"

She was silent.

Charlie stared back at her and wondered who would blink first and how long it would take. He noticed her eye makeup was still intact, her hair was wild, and her lipstick was smeared on the left side.

Heather raised her hands as far as she could, and then lowered her face so she could scratch her nose.

Detective Hall lost his temper. He pounded the table with his fist. "Answer his question, now. Do you hear me?"

Heather turned her head toward Hall, her face expressionless. "You will speak to me in a civil tongue." She turned her focus back to Charlie.

Hall sat back stunned, not the response he had expected.

"Heather, there's no need to pretend you don't know what happened or that you're innocent. All I want to know is why?"

She cocked her head slightly to the right, then toward the left, then straightened her head and blinked a few times.

Charlie thought she resembled a hawk studying its prey. He sighed heavily, leaned forward, rested his forearms on the table, his palms flat on the table.

Her eyes shifted downward at his torn blood-stained shirtsleeve. "I never meant to harm you, but you got in my way." Heather pointed her chin at Officer Thayer. "Don't ever grab me like that again."

There were no emotions in her words. Her tone was calm and matter-of-fact.

Thayer's response was as dead as hers, complete silence without a glance toward her direction.

"Heather, why did you kill your mother? Your birth mother." Charlie decided to go ahead.

A sliver of a smile turned her lips. "You found her."

"Right where you left her."

"I bet she was a sight by now." Her tongue flicked out to moisten her lips.

"Why did you kill her?"

"Why not? She didn't want me. I didn't want her. My father didn't want her. Nobody in this world wanted her."

Charlie saw a dangerous mind in that small head. "That's no reason to kill her."

She shrugged slightly. "I think of it like thinning the herd, getting the vermin population under control."

"But I'm confused, why kill her now?"

"My father moved to Georgia. I was bored hunting alone. So I went after something more thrilling. I tracked her down. She wasn't that easy to find, but the kill was."

Detective Hall mumbled. "You're damn insane."

"Hmm, maybe, but I don't think so."

Charlie tugged his earlobe. He agreed with Hall. The girl was not right in the head. Not at all. "So is that why you killed Mitch and Candi? For the thrill of it?"

"May I have some water?" She looked at Thayer. "Please, sir."

Thayer looked at Charlie. "Ask someone to get her some."

Thayer stepped out and returned in a matter of seconds with Heather's water then set on the table within her reach.

She picked up the cup, dipped her head, and then drank. "Thank you. No, I didn't kill them for sport if that's what you mean. I decided to see if Candi knew she had a little sister."

Heather sighed softly. "I always wanted a big sister." She stared at nothing for a moment, then wobbled her head and picked at her fingernails. "Anyway, I tracked her down easy enough. Long story short, Candi said mother had mentioned me once. She said mother came home early one day and caught her in bed with a boy. Candi said while mother beat her mercilessly, she said, '*I knew I'd kept the wrong daughter.*'"

Heather laughed. "She kept the wrong one, like she picked one of us from a litter of puppies." She tapped her fingertips on the table. "Where was I? Oh, yeah. I snuck into Ken's Playhouse through the back door. At first Candi didn't believe I was her sister. But I convinced her to listen to my story. Candi said it sounded like something her mother would do. Candi was glad to meet me. She said she wanted us to be sisters, real sisters, but we couldn't because of Mitch. He wouldn't like me hanging around. She told me if I got rid of him, then she'd be in control of his business, and we could be close like sisters should be."

Charlie thought Heather was too clever than to trust Candi. The need to be wanted blinded her judgement. "So you believed her?"

"Yes. Candi and I made a deal. She told me about Mitch's plan to meet Joan at The Primrose in three weeks. So I conned Miss Delaney into giving me a job. They always fall for the poor single mother just trying to feed her baby routine. It got me out of plenty of jams." Heather smiled at her brilliant disguise.

"But how did Candi know beforehand Mitch was going to meet Miss Delaney in the woods?"

Heather grinned. "Ah, that was pure dumb luck. Originally, Candi was going to lure him outside. We were going to make it look like a robbery gone horribly wrong. But then I overheard Miss Delaney arguing with Mitch. I pinched her knife and the rest you know." She sat back and sighed happily.

Chill bumps crawled over Charlie's arms as Heather snickered gleefully. She's reliving the kill and enjoying it, he thought. "I guess you killed Candi because she backed out of your deal?"

Charlie's question brought Heather back to the present. She frowned. "A liar just like mother. Candi was embarrassed by me, the ugly, scrawny sister. She never intended for us to be a family. So I did the only thing I could do. I killed her. She forced me. I couldn't have her pinning Mitch's murder on me. And I took her money. I mean why not? It's not like she needed it. She was dead."

Heather smiled slightly. "It was kind of sad though, watching her die. She was surprised that I did it. But I think what upset her most wasn't the fact that I plunged the scissors into her neck." Heather shook her head. "No, it was the fact she was bleeding all over her fancy nightgown. Candi tried to pull it away from the trailing blood, but she died before she could prevent it."

Charlie rubbed his chin as he thought about Heather's statement. "So you knew about your fingerprints, didn't you? That's why you never mentioned anything about wiping away your prints."

Detective Hall inhaled sharply. "So that's what the intake officer was complaining about. Well, in all my years, I've never run across someone like you."

"What, a freak? Yeah, I knew about it, but it's been a blessing … until now." Her tongue ran around her cheek. "How did you figure it out?"

Officer Thayer quickly answered. "He's a dadgum genius."

Heather looked at Officer Thayer. "So Tonto can speak."

Charlie knocked on the table. "Let's get back to the investigation. You know, I can understand why you think you had to kill your mother, Mitch, and Candi. Your mother abandoned you like a dog at the pound. She didn't want you. You thought Mitch prevented your relationship with your half-sister, a relationship you desperately wanted. But then you figured out Candi lied to you. She used you to get what she wanted, and then tossed you aside like your mother did." Charlie hunched up his shoulder. "But why did you want to harm Miss Delaney? Why did you want her to take the blame for Mitch's murder? I mean she never lied to you or cheated you or used you. She gave you a job and treated you with respect. By all accounts she's a fair boss. None better. So why?"

For the first time, Heather seemed upset. "I don't know."

"What do you mean you don't know? You had reasons to kill the others. So why Miss Delaney?"

She stared at her hands lying on the table.

"Surely you know. Tell me."

Heather shook her head.

Charlie slammed his fist on the table. "Tell me, Heather. Tell me!"

Her lips trembled. "Because …because." Heather looked up at the ceiling and started to cry. "I was jealous."

"Jealous? I don't understand."

"Yes, jealous!" In a mocking voice, Heather said, "Everybody adores her. Everybody thinks she's God's gift to womankind. And

Andrew …" She bent her head to wipe her cheeks and nose. "He worships her."

"So you're in love with Andrew?" Charlie didn't think Heather was capable of that emotion, then he remembered her grandmother telling him about Robert Sorrows the pretend but real boyfriend.

"No!" Heather laughed nervously.

"What about Robert Sorrows? You were in love with him and he abandoned you. Didn't he?"

Heather held her breath as she thought about her true feelings for her high school friend. Her breath rushed out. "Yes, but it wasn't like you think. He loved me too but like a sister. You see … well … he couldn't love me any other way."

Charlie understood. "He was gay."

She nodded.

"So he was your family, the brother you never had. And when he joined the army and never came back, how did that make you feel?"

Heather clasped her hands. Her knuckles lost their color. "Why should he come back? It's not like we had any kind of a future together."

"It didn't make you angry that one day he was your best friend and then poof," Charlie made exploding hands, "he was gone?"

"Okay, yes, it made me mad. But why should I have expected anything more?" Heather gritted her teeth.

Charlie wanted to understand Heather's lack of compassion. "What about your grandparents?"

"What about them?" Heather still squeezing her hands together, began to rock slowly.

"Do you love them?"

"They're my grandparents."

"But do you love them?"

"Yeah, as much as they love me. Granddad had a car accident when I was two. Scrabbled his brains. Grandma spends most of her time caring for him."

"Who took care of you?"

"She fed me and made sure I had clean clothes."

Charlie almost felt sorry for her. She never seemed to have any kind of physical relationship. "Did you ever sit in her lap while she read a story to you?"

"No, of course not. She didn't have time for that kind of stuff."

"But your father did, right?"

Heather smiled. "Dad would take me hunting and fishing. I learned to appreciate the thrill of the hunt." Her eyes seemed to sparkle.

"He taught me everything about the forest. How to sneak up on someone without them hearing you. He taught me how to survive in the woods by myself. He said I shouldn't depend on nobody. Always look out for number one."

As she released her hands, the color rushed back into her knuckles. "He showed me the sweet spot on a deer's neck to bleed it." Heather leaned forward so she could slide her index finger across her throat. "Right, here."

Charlie remembered that was the same spot she slid the knife across Mitch's throat. "Did your father drink a lot?"

Heather nodded. "He had to. He hurt a lot and he had to quiet the alien voices in his head."

"Do you hear alien voices?" Charlie wondered if she was schizophrenic, too.

"No, they only talk to dad."

"Hmm, I see. Where does your dad live now?" Charlie hoped she might be caught off guard.

Heather grinned. "Oh, you think you're so smart." She shook a boney finger at him. "I can't tell you. Dad said it's just our secret."

Charlie laughed. "Well, you got me didn't you?"

"I'm smarter than I look."

"You love your father a lot?"

"Yes. He's always been there for me."

"You'd do anything for him, right?" Charlie saw more pieces of the puzzle come together,

Heather nodded.

"You killed your mother not for only abandoning you but for your father as well. Didn't you?"

"It's her fault! Dad didn't hear the aliens until she did him wrong, lying and cheating on him. She got him to drinking and all. She was a horrible, evil, cruel woman. The voices got worse. I thought if I got rid of her they might go away."

"But they didn't, did they?"

Heather whispered, "No."

"Is that the real reason you killed Candi? You thought she might be causing the voices."

"Tut, that's just stupid." Heather hung her head and mumbled, "You're dumber than you look." She looked up at Charlie. "I told you that Candi and I had a plan and she double crossed me." She shook her head. "I did what dad taught me. Looked out for number one. So I killed her."

Charlie shifted gears. "Let's get back to Miss Delaney and Andrew."

Heather smirked as if there was a bad taste in her mouth.

"You are jealous of Miss Delaney because she's everything you'd like to be. Beautiful, successful, smart, and the one thing you covet most; she is loved by everyone without even trying. Everybody wants to be her friend. Everybody!"

Heather bristled. "I'm smart! I'm not stupid! I'm just as smart as her!"

Charlie ignored her outburst. "Everybody included Andrew. He loved her, too. He'd do anything for her. Miss Delaney had his love and devotion. And you had nothing from him. He just couldn't see past your scrawny, unattractive self. He couldn't see how smart you are. Andrew was blinded by Miss Delaney's beauty. So when you saw the chance to get her out of your way, you took it. Because you're smart. You always look out for number one. Yeah?"

Heather's chest heaved. "Yes, I wanted her gone! Women like her make men crazy. They ruin them!"

"Like your mother did to your dad."

251

"Yes! I was trying to save him! Can't you understand that? To save him!"

Charlie nodded. "I see. You just care about his well-being."

"Yes!"

Detective Hall grunted, "You're so thoughtful."

Heather scowled at him.

Charlie shifted in his chair, placed his right arm on the table, then leaned forward and asked softly, "Tell me something, Heather, why did you kill them the way you did? Up close and personal." Charlie could see her emotion shift from agitation to one of pleasure.

"I enjoyed the look of terror on their faces. They were afraid of me. The scraggily girl they never gave a second thought."

"Made you feel powerful, yeah?"

"Yeah, I suppose so."

"But what about Mitch? You didn't see his face."

"No, but I manipulated him like Candi. He just sat there moaning with pleasure as I stroked his greasy head."

"So that made you feel … what?"

Heather tilted her head side to side as she thought about it. "I guess, mmm … maybe … pretty?"

Charlie choked. "Pretty? You slit a man's throat and that makes you feel pretty?" The girl is sick, beyond sick, he thought. "You're going to have to explain that to me."

She sighed softly. "He was moaning, telling me how good it felt. My touch made him excited. You know, sexually." Heather sighed again.

Charlie felt a wave of nausea and swallowed it away. He wanted this interview to be over but he had one more question. "Now, tell me how setting up Miss Delaney made you feel."

"Like her master. She had no control of what was happening to her. I would see her suffer for a long time, maybe even die in jail. Either way, she'd no longer be capable of ruining good men." Heather held up her hands as high as she could, and then wiggled her fingers. "She was my puppet. Dance little monkey. Dance—."

Charlie interrupted her. He was furious at what she had done to Joan. Almost destroyed her because of some warped sense of self and retribution. Her need to be the savior of a boy she barely knew.

"Did you see Spanky the night you killed Candi?"

Heather seemed dazed by the sudden shift in questioning. She blinked repeatedly as she thought about Charlie's question. "Yes, I was there. It's easy for me to hide in the shadows. I think I spooked him when he left Candi's dressing room." Heather giggled.

Charlie wondered if she giggled because she relished the fact she had scared Spanky or because she was reliving Candi's death. Both creeped him out.

"You went after Spanky because you overheard Miss Delaney tell me he knew who killed Mitch, didn't you? Always looking out for number one. Yeah?"

Heather nodded. "I thought I was in the clear. I had to get rid of him."

"Why didn't you leave town after you killed Candi?"

Heather shrugged. "Like I said." She looked at Thayer. "I thought y'all were too stupid to figure it out. I wanted to witness the demise of the beloved Miss Delaney."

"Pfft." Officer Thayer was disgusted by her response.

Charlie chuckled. "It appears you're the stupid one. Spanky lied to Miss Delaney. If only you hadn't stuck around for a boy who couldn't care less about you. Andrew didn't want your help. He never needed you. Never wanted you. Andrew had no use for you at all." He smiled as he watched her face contort with fury. "Some boy made you forget about number one. Some boy made you stupid."

Heather lunged at Charlie. The handcuffs chained to the table kept her from her target: Charlie's neck. "No! You bastard! I'm not stupid! He needs me. You men are all stupid. Stupid! All of you!"

Two officers entered the room.

"Take her away."

Charlie heard her screams fade as they dragged her down the hallway. "I'm not stupid!"

Chapter 25

Officer Thayer and Charlie entered the station. Penny, the dayshift receptionist was long gone. They were greeted by Derek, a retired pro football player. He didn't see much playing time, but it wasn't due to his lack of size. "Chief, I don't get to see you much and now, twice this week. What brings you in at this time of night?"

"Same case, and boy am I beat."

Derek noticed the dark red stain on his sleeve, and then he saw Thayer's chest. "Holy cow, what happened to you two?"

Officer Thayer answered. "You remember that skinny, little girl we brought in with the stripper and the two guys?"

"She did that to y'all?"

"Yep, he's telling the truth, Derek." Charlie confirmed Thayer's story.

"That's crazy, man." Derek shook his head in disbelief.

"She's the crazy one. The girl's a psycho." Thayer replied as he followed Charlie into the inter sanctum of the station.

"I'm too tired to take the steps. Let's catch the elevator." Charlie leaned against the wall as they waited for the doors to slide open.

"What's Missus McClung going to think about your injury?"

Charlie heard the ding of the elevator announcing its arrival. "She's not going to be happy, I can tell you that. Once I change shirts, Marian won't have a clue anything happened."

They stepped inside.

"I'm going to make sure she sees I'm okay before I tell her."

They exited the elevator. Only one officer was on the floor. Willard. His head popped up when he heard Charlie's voice.

"Officer Willard what are you still doing here?"

"Crap! What happened to you guys?" Willard pushed away from his desk and met Charlie and Thayer in the hallway outside of Charlie's office.

"We had a minor mishap with one of our suspects, Heather."

Willard pointed to Thayer's chest. "Looks like someone ripped out your heart. I never thought you had one."

Thayer sneered. "You're so funny."

"Answer my question, Willard. Why are you still here? I thought you were supposed to be at The Primrose."

"Sir, it's after midnight. The Primrose closes at nine o'clock on Tuesday. Officer Marshall took everyone home to your house. Your father told me to go home. He said he could handle inside the house. I came back here to finish up some paperwork."

"Sorry, I've lost all track of time. Is Marshall still at the house?"

"No, sir, Officer Dodson relieved him."

"Good. Anything to report?"

"No, chief. Everything is right as rain."

Charlie pressed the heels of his hands against his eyes. "Go home, Willard. The paperwork can wait."

"Thank you, sir." Willard walked back to his desk to file away the papers scattered on top.

Charlie patted Thayer on his good shoulder. "It's time for you to hit the road home, too."

"Are you sure, sir?"

"Yeah, I'm going to change shirts and go home."

"Okay, goodnight. I'll see you in a few hours."

Charlie walked into his office and shut the door. He sat at his desk and stared at Marian's picture. He wondered how she would react to his injury. They had had a long discussion about his job before they were married. Ma said she had told Marian what it was like being married to a copper. Marian had accepted all the warts and moles that came with his job.

He changed shirts and neatly folded the damaged one. If Marian was like Ma, it would be, '*Save the buttons and I can make cleaning rags out of the material*'. Charlie smiled at one of his childhood memories of Ma ripping apart one of Da's ruined shirts.

The alarm clock blasted Charlie awake. Before going to bed, he changed the awake time from five-thirty to seven-thirty, and was now wishing he hadn't set it all. He rolled over to spoon Marian, but she was already up. She didn't know about his arm. By the time he arrived home, the house was quiet. Everyone had gone to bed. Marian had left a note on the kitchen counter, apologizing for not waiting up. She was bone tired, and keep banging her head on the kitchen table from falling asleep.

Charlie lay in the bed and listened to the sounds of Marian trying to be quiet. She still hadn't quite mastered the art of silence. He could smell the aroma of coffee. Its lure was overpowering and he decided to get out of bed. He threw on a robe for two reasons: Ma didn't like half naked people in the kitchen and he didn't want Marian to see his stitches.

He strolled into the kitchen. Marian sat at the kitchen table reading the morning paper. A cup of coffee sat at arm's reach. Instead of sneaking up behind her and wrapping his arm around her, Charlie whispered loudly, "Good morning, love."

Marian jumped up and they met half way. "What time did you get home? I didn't even hear you get into bed."

Charlie kissed her nose. "Close to one o'clock. I was extra quiet. I didn't want to wake you." So far, so good, he thought.

"What would you like for breakfast?" She asked as she poured him a cup of coffee.

"Eggs, bacon, and toast will be fine." With cup in hand, Charlie walked over to the table and glanced down at the paper. "Anything interesting?"

"One thing of interest." She open the refrigerator and collected the ingredients for scrambled eggs. "Would you like a ham and cheese omelet?"

"That would hit the spot." He sipped his coffee. "Hmm, good coffee. What was the interesting story?"

Marian cracked a few eggs into a large mixing bowl. "Some cop had his left forearm slashed open."

Charlie froze. He swallowed hard, and then turned to face the music. "Yeah? Hmm, did it happen to mention his name?"

"Charles Patrick McClung, did you really think you could get by without telling me?" Marian stood with her feet apart and her fists on her hips.

Charlie swore he saw horns pop out of her head. "Honestly, I was going to tell you. I didn't want you to worry. I wanted you to see I was okay before I told you." He sat down his cup, approached his wife, and stopped a foot in front of her. "Honestly, I was going to tell you."

Marian smiled and playfully slapped his shoulder. "Fine. The look on your face is penance enough. I've never seen your Adam's apple bob as much as it did just now." She stood on her tip toes and looked at his head. "Are you sweating?"

His hand felt his forehead. "Yeah, you scared me to death with that …" Charlie pointed at her face, "demon face."

Marian grabbed his finger and pulled him to the kitchen table. "Sit down. Now, let me see that arm."

He placed his arm on the table. "How did you know, really?"

"I saw your arm when I got up this morning. You had it slung over my hip." She sat beside him and studied the cut. "Who did this to you?"

"Heather."

Marian gasped. "Heather?" She picked up his arm and planted kisses around the stitches. "Does it hurt?"

"Not anymore." Charlie grinned as he leaned in to kiss her.

"Blimey, son!" Da and Ma stood over them.

Charlie finished his kiss before addressing his parents. "Good, you're both here. Now I'll only have to tell the story once."

"Wait. Everyone sit at the counter." Marian ordered. "You tell us what happened while I make breakfast."

Marian and Charlie sat in the living room drinking coffee while Ma and Da cleaned up the breakfast dishes.

Charlie cradled Marian under his right arm and kissed the top of her head. "I'll need to go into the office for a while to write up the report and whatnot."

"I know. Maybe you could meet us for lunch at the Chinese restaurant?"

He squeezed her with his good arm. "Let's call it a plan." Charlie looked at the mantle clock. "It's nine o'clock now. It shouldn't take long, I'll meet you around one o'clock?"

Marian kissed his cheek. "Sounds good to me."

Da yelled from the kitchen. "Son, where do ya keep the trash bags?"

Charlie released Marian. "Coming, Da."

He walked into the laundry room and changed the garbage bag.

Da picked up the full bag. "I'll take it to the can, son. Go back to Marian."

Charlie took the bag from Da's hand. "I've got this. Besides, Marian is helping Ma make something, scones probably."

"I'll go with ya then." Da followed Charlie to the back door.

"We're baking scones for Charlie's office and they'll be ready soon so don't be on the doss." Ma warned her husband.

Marian's forehead wrinkled. "What does that mean, *on the doss*?"

Ma's laughter filled the room. "I forget ya not be familiar with our Irish slang. It means, goofing off."

Marian grinned and yelled after her husband. "No on the doss!"

Holding up her flour covered hands, Ma leaned toward her daughter-in-law and kissed her on the cheek. "That's my girl."

Charlie and Da waved their hands at their wives, acknowledging their orders, continued out the back door, and then strolled down the flagstone path to the far corner of the backyard where the garbage bin was hidden inside a pergola.

"Marian has a beautiful garden." Da surveyed the backyard.

Charlie stood with Da outside of the pergola. "I swear, Da, she could shove a dead stick in the ground and it would sprout fruit."

Da laughed. "Sounds like ya Ma." He slapped his son on the back. "We got us some fine women, that we have."

Charlie grinned. "Yeah, that we do."

"Son, what's that in front of the gate?"

Charlie threw the garbage into the bin, and then walked to the spot where his father was pointing. The hair on Charlie's neck stood up, his heart pounded against his chest, and goosebumps broke out over his body.

It was a misshapen heart made out of bits of paper.

The End

About The Author

I am the author of The Charlie McClung mysteries, including *Brilliant Disguise*, *A Good Girl*, and *Criminal Kind*. I live in Georgia with my husband of 35+ years and our Tuxedo cat named Gertrude.

Thank you for taking the time to read *Sins of My Youth*. If you enjoyed it, please consider telling your friends and posting a short review on Amazon and Goodreads. Word of mouth and reviews are an author's best friends and are very much appreciated.

The fifth book in the series, *Flirting with Time*, will be released in at the end of 2016.

You can find me on Facebook, Pinterest, LinkedIn, Goodreads, Google+, Wiselike, and Twitter. I invite you to visit my website:

www.MaryAnneEdwards.com

Charlie and Marian look forward to seeing you again as they journey together through mystery, murder, and love.